Let the Rain Fall

Enjoy the story!

Rachel S. Norby

RACHEL NORBY

authorHOUSE®

AuthorHouse™
1663 Liberty Drive
Bloomington, IN 47403
www.authorhouse.com
Phone: 1-800-839-8640

First published by AuthorHouse   12/13/2010

ISBN: 978-1-4520-9487-8 (hc)
ISBN: 978-1-4520-9488-5 (sc)
ISBN: 978-1-4520-9489-2 (e)

Library of Congress Control Number: 2010916069

Printed in the United States of America

This book is printed on acid-free paper.

Certain stock imagery © Thinkstock.

For my family and friends,
who always support me in every endeavor

We are most alive when we're in love.
  -*John Updike*

PROLOGUE

THE DEEP HUM of the basses resonated in the damp air as the last few people filed into the small clearing. Katherine had been there for hours already. She had wandered down the small dirt path early in the morning, finally settling in on her favorite bench with a blanket wrapped around her to keep out the chill. The bench had been built years ago just for her, and as she sat on it, she began to reminisce. She consciously allowed her mind to wander, relishing in every remembrance, drinking it all in. Some of her fondest memories had happened in this very spot. She let her eyes slowly pass over every little part of the clearing, their clearing, trying to remember everything just as it had all happened, trying not to forget. She never wanted to forget.

She had been lost in her reverie when the preacher arrived, followed shortly after by the choir, and finally her friends and family. It was a relatively small party. Katherine had expected this, due to the fact that she had been an only child and her parents had died years ago, and most of the few close friends that they had had passed away in recent years. Her brother-in-law, John, squeezed her arm as he passed by. She gave him a weary smile, and then turned her attention to the choir as they sang her favorite hymn.

The song performed its magic once again on Katherine, reaching her in a way she couldn't quite put into words. She had always marveled at the power of music: its ability to alter moods, uplift, and in this case, heal. She closed her eyes and felt the song, rather than listened to it, as the choir came to the last climactic refrain:

Let the rain fall down,
Let the rain fall down,
Let the rain
Fall from Heaven.

It had been misting all morning, and, ironically, as the choir finished the song, it began to rain softly. Multiple umbrellas went up simultaneously as the preacher stepped out from his place within the choir and made his way down to the middle of the crowd. Katherine mused that the weather always seemed to be morbid on the days of funerals. It was as if God himself sent a signal to Mother Nature to make the weather match people's moods. She didn't mind. Katherine had always loved the rain. Though she had her umbrella along, she let the rain run freely down her face. It was a form of catharsis for her.

Katherine knew it was unusual to have a choir sing at a funeral, but then again, she wasn't one to care much about what people thought. Not recently anyways. There had been a time when she cared, so very long ago, but that had caused her to make the biggest mistake of her life. Never again, she had vowed, never again.

Katherine shed not one tear throughout the entire funeral. Even as she watched the coffin lowered into the freshly-dug grave, no tears came. It wasn't that she hadn't loved; she had loved more deeply than words could express. It was simply that Katherine realized that she had been given a second chance at love; a chance that was more than she deserved. Much more than she had deserved.

CHAPTER ONE

KATHERINE SAT UPON the edge of her bed and looked one last time at what used to be her home. She had put it up for sale a week ago, and the house had sold within a few days. She knew that it would. She had asked far less than it was worth, partly because money didn't really matter to her at this point in her life, and partly because she had just wanted to sell it quickly.

It had always been her and Will's home, and now that he was gone, she couldn't see living in it anymore. Every nook and cranny held some memory for her. Memories of him. Memories of them together. Probably far more than most couples, since they had designed the house together, and inlaid in every brick and piece of lumber was their sweat and toil. The house was charming, even to the outsider; this was certain. But it held far more of a charm for Katherine, since she knew the story behind every part of the home. For instance, the outsider would never know that the painting room was designed as a surprise for Katherine by Will. The outsider wouldn't know that the whole wall of windows in the room were put there because Katherine loved nature and loved to paint what she saw beyond the glass.

The outsider wouldn't know that Will and Katherine had laid the rugged brick on the patio by themselves, even though they had more than enough money to have someone else do it, and that one of the bricks was just a shade off color with "I love Katherine" carved into it. The outsider also wouldn't know how many hours Will had spent in bed that last year with Katherine by his side, the very bed on which Katherine now sat, trying to keep him comfortable and happy before his impending death. The outsider wouldn't know.

That morning, as Katherine had walked around the grounds and then made her way into the house, she filed it all away in her memory. One comfort to her was that she had their house depicted in a painting she had created in between packing and running errands the past few weeks. She had captured many things in this painting, due partly to her obvious mastery of the medium and partly to the emotion that was tied into it. She captured the way the house was situated atop a hill overlooking the grove of trees that held their clearing; the little dirt path that led up the hill to the front porch, surrounded by flowers on both sides; the roughness in the stone that covered the outside of the entire house; the large windows, each with a wooden flowerbox filled with a variety of vibrant flowers beneath it; the little stone chimney jutting out of the roof that they used in the wintertime to help keep warm. She had also captured the warmth that radiated from the home, despite it being made out of stone, with the hues of paint that she so effectively chose. The sun seemed to not only shine down on the home, but flow out of the home as well. This painting she would take with her and hang in her new room, a constant reminder of a life built together.

Before Will died, Katherine had painted something for him as well. She had crafted multiple paintings for him throughout their relationship, but this one was unique in the fact that it would be given to him as a parting gift. It was an unusual painting, but not because of the way she painted it; it was a basic oil painting not unique in any stylistic sort of way. It was unusual because of the subject matter. It was a bed. She had painted it the way it looked in the morning, with the covers strewn across the top and the sun coming in the east window, illuminating everything in the room. Since the room was mostly white, it almost seemed to glow. Katherine attempted to capture all of the memories that their bed held. The bed held many; not only of love-making, but of long talks deep into the night, laughter, and also pain—the pain of watching someone you love die slowly before your eyes. For this, she used some dark hues within the recesses of the covers that were a sharp contrast to the rest of the painting.

She knew it was the best painting she had ever done, not only by her own assessment of her work after she was finished, but by the reaction her husband had given her. Usually, Will was able to express himself easily. Though he was not a big talker, he always seemed to have the gift of having the right words for every situation. For this, he had none. He just looked at the painting for minutes on end, driving Katherine to the edge of insanity wondering what exactly he was thinking. Finally, almost childlike, she had blurted out, "Do you like it?"

Will hadn't answered right away. He continued to look at the painting for a few moments longer, and then replied, "I'd like to take this with me when I die. It's the most..." he searched for the right words. "It's perfect...just like my Kate." Then, he had kissed her forehead, her favorite spot to be kissed, and had fallen back asleep. He had slept through the night, and then never woke up. The painting had been placed in his coffin with him.

This is what Katherine recalled as she sat upon the edge of the bed. It's strange what sitting on a bed can make you remember.

Chapter Two

Katherine and Will had made a plan together shortly before he had died. This entailed the sale of their extended property far beyond the grove of trees, the building of a unique sort of assisted living home on that property, and the understanding that Katherine would move into that building as soon as Will passed away. The land had sold within a month and the building put up within three months, with residents moving in a few months before Will's death. The time had now come for Katherine to move in as well.

Katherine brought very few belongings with her when she moved; the few she had consisted of her bed, her recently finished painting of their old home, an old easy chair that didn't look like much but had formed to her body over the years, her wardrobe, some painting supplies, and some basic living necessities. All else she had either sold with the house or given away. She had no need for such things anymore.

New Horizons, the name the assisted living home had adopted, had sent a truck to Katherine's home, just a jaunt up the road, to get her belongings for her. Though she didn't have much to bring to her new home, she was grateful for the help.

The truth was, the few friends who hadn't either moved away or passed away were too old to help with such things.

It wasn't that she felt that old; her 75 years of age she wore quite gracefully and was still considered a beautiful woman by many. Somehow the wrinkles that plagued most people had not found a home in her face, she still had a nice figure from regular exercise, and she had amazing emerald eyes that seemed to hold both beauty and wisdom at the same time. Will had always told her that her eyes "held the secrets of the universe." She never really believed him, but she had always liked the way it made her feel when he said it.

As her belongings were moved into her room, Katherine felt grateful for many other things as well. She was exceptionally thankful that her room had a large window facing northward, where she could see her grove of trees that held their clearing about one-half a mile away. This was the only portion of her property that she did not sell, nor did she ever intend to sell. Not only did the grove hold many memories for Katherine, but it now contained Will's gravestone as well. This was the place she would walk to faithfully each day to visit her Will.

Though Katherine didn't know any of the residents yet, she was also thankful that she'd have some company in this last leg of her life. She had always enjoyed the company of others, and she knew it wouldn't be good for her to be living on her own. She still had one good friend in town, Gloria, with whom she would have considered living, but her husband was still alive and doing well. Maybe Gloria would join her at another time.

Katherine also felt she had something to offer the residents of New Horizons. She wasn't exactly sure exactly what it was, but somehow she had been felt a sort of peace about this being the place she wanted to be and the place she was supposed to be at this point in her life.

Katherine was also incredibly grateful for New Horizons

and the freedom that it offered its residents. It was actually more like a miniature apartment complex than anything else, with each living area equipped with everything an independent person would need: a kitchenette, a living room, a bathroom, and a bedroom. Residents could make their own meals in their place if they wished, or they could inform the kitchen staff a day ahead of time which meals they wished to eat in the commons area so that they could socialize with the other residents. They could do their own laundry or choose to have it done by the staff. In short, the residents could ask for as little or as much help as they needed. This was the agreement Katherine and Will had made with the land purchasers, and in exchange for that agreement the buyers were given a very low price. Only the owners of New Horizons knew who Katherine was and of her involvement in the development of the assisted living home; all of the other residents simply saw her as the new resident moving in and someone who sparked their curiosity.

Three such people whose curiosity was definitely sparked by the new resident happened to be three sisters who had been at New Horizons since the day it opened. They were three somewhat eccentric ladies who had decided that they wanted to go out of this life living together. Their rooms were adjacent to each other, and though they slept in separate rooms, they convened each morning for breakfast in the commons area and often stayed there until bedtime. Their favorite pastimes were knitting, telling stories about their past life, and, of course, gossiping about the present. The latter was what they now convened in doing as they saw the graceful figure of Katherine make her way out of her room and into the hallway.

"Who do you suppose she is?" the oldest sister, Nicene, said to her younger two sisters as they all put down their knitting projects.

"I have no idea. Why do you think I would know any more than you do?" retorted the middle sister, Patience.

"Oh, I do hope that she'll be someone who likes to mingle! Or even better, knit!" replied the youngest sister, Hope, with eyes wide.

None of them had a chance to meet Katherine or say anything to her, as Katherine walked past the reception counter and out the front door.

CHAPTER THREE

KATHERINE KNEW THAT she should introduce herself to the residents sometime within the day lest they think her a snob, but she knew there'd be time for that at dinner when most of the residents would be out and about. Right now, she needed to get some fresh air and walk to the grove to clear her mind. She walked across the street that had been created when New Horizons was built, and she mused how this very street used to be a field that she owned just months ago.

After walking on the grassy field for a bit, she quickened her pace as she neared the grove of trees. Since she habitually walked at least two miles daily, this half-a-mile walk seemed easy for her. She rarely approached the grove from this side; usually, she'd be coming down the little dirt path from her house into the clearing. It seemed almost for a moment not to be the grove that she knew so well. Once she made her way past the first set of trees and could see the clearing, however, the air of familiarity settled on her as she took a seat on her bench.

For a while, Kate sat mesmerized, staring at the gravestone that lay not ten feet from her. The gravestone read,

William Michael Brenner
February 3, 1925-April 25, 2001
Man of faith, courage, and heart.
Loving husband and friend.

Katherine hadn't really known what to put as the epitaph on the gravestone. How does one put into words what a person's life has meant? Can it be put into words at all? Does it somehow make a life seem smaller by attempting to capture one's entire being in a few words?

She had decided to go with the words she felt best captured who Will had been. He had definitely been a man of faith. Ever since Katherine had known him, even when they were young, he had always had a steady head about him and an unwavering faith in God. He also had incredible faith in people. Katherine could remember times where she wasn't sure of herself, and every time she turned around, Will was there to encourage her with his unfaltering faith in her abilities.

He had always been a man of great courage and heart as well. He had been in World War II during the last leg of it, and for his bravery had received multiple medals. She also recalled one of her most painful memories from her marriage with Will… the difficulty she had getting pregnant. It took years for her to finally get pregnant, and when she did, the baby had died at childbirth. It had been a boy. The doctors later told her she would never again have children. Though Katherine knew this must have hurt Will, he never blamed her nor did he ever bring it up again. He just held Katherine when she cried every night for the next two months, murmuring to her how he loved her and knew they would make it through this. Her heart had eventually healed, and she had forever marveled at how Will's heart had helped to heal hers.

Katherine wasn't sure how long she had been sitting there

when she snapped out of her reverie. She slowly reached down into her sweater pocket to take out a poem she had written. Though she usually preferred painting as her mode for expressing herself, she would write poems every once in a while when she felt like the painting muses weren't giving her much inspiration for the day. Some poems that she had written for Will in the past she would sneak into his jacket pocket or under his pillow, or some such place that he would find it at some point during the day. She had always tried to spy on him so that when he found it, she could see his facial expressions. He would usually look surprised as his fingers touched something unknown, and then his face would slowly register a faint smile as he figured out what it was. He would find a spot to sit or lean against to read what she had written, his eyes lighting up in certain places or his smile widening at certain lines. He then would look around, as if he knew she were spying on him, but by that time, she would usually be gone.

She painfully thought of the fact that she wouldn't be able to see his facial expressions now. Despite that, she took solace in the feeling that somehow, some way, he was able to hear her and would have a smile on his face. Somehow God would allow her that. She read the words out loud, hoping that they were somehow traversing upward across the abyss of the unknown:

My love, my life,
my Will…
You have been my will
to believe in myself,
My will to go on
when heartache darkened my door,
My will to believe in a God
that would take a child from my bosom,
My Will to love

For eternity.
There's something about love
that never dies,
Though a body is laid to rest,
your love lingers...
and so does mine.

As Katherine finished reading the last line, she felt a wave of loneliness wash over her. She wanted to feel his touch, to hear his voice. *'No,'* she thought, *'not now...I have been so strong...'* And then, for the first time since Will's death, Katherine let herself cry.

Chapter Four

IT WAS JUST before dinner when Katherine walked back into the front door of New Horizons. She hoped that her eyes weren't too puffy from her visit to the grove. She didn't want her first impression to be one of a sad, lonely old woman.

As she walked in and scanned the commons room, she noticed three women very involved in their knitting projects. Despite the ordeal she had just been through, she found the scene in front of her to be strangely comical. One woman had a large gray bun pinned neatly to the back of her head, and she was bragging about her grandson and his recent little league game. Another, who had dyed brown hair that was very short and stylish for someone of her age, was nodding and "um-humming" along to the other woman's story to show that she was listening. The third woman, with unruly locks of grayish-colored hair stemming out from her head, looked incredibly frustrated with her sewing project and was pulling on her strings to undo a mistake she had made. She butted in on the bun woman's story and said, "Well, I know you think your grandson is impressive, Nicey, but you have to admit you're a little biased.

Listening to you, you'd think your little Tommy was going to make it to the big leagues!" She was going to add something else, but then she caught Katherine's eye as she was walking past. She coughed loudly to let her other sisters know they should look up as well.

"Oh, you ladies needn't stop your knitting or your little league story. I was just walking to my room," Katherine apologized. She had wanted to rest and freshen up a bit before coming back out to the commons for dinner and meeting everybody. Since they were already stopped, she decided it was as good of time as any to introduce herself. "I'm Katherine, by the way. I live in the corner room down the hall." She nodded her head in the direction of her room.

"Oh, lovely to meet you! My name is Hope, and these are my two sisters. We live in rooms C, D, and E," the lady with the short, dyed brown hair energetically offered. She was about to say that she was the youngest sister when she was interrupted by the crazy-haired sister.

"And I'm Patience, the nearly-forgotten middle sister," she said dramatically, and then added, "and the brightest of the three sisters." She nestled back into her chair and resumed her knitting with a slightly smug look on her face. Katherine almost laughed out loud.

"You mean IMPatience. That's what Mother should have named you," scolded the one who Katherine assumed must be the oldest sister. "My name is Nicene, but everyone here calls me Aunt Nicey, or just plain Nicey." She smiled warmly at Katherine and then continued on, "My mother wanted to name us all after qualities that she thought every Christian woman should possess, so she gave us somewhat unique names. She had originally wanted to give me a name that had to do with love, but couldn't make a name out of it. So, she just picked another quality that was like love, being nice to people, and made my name Nicene. She's always called me Nicey, and the name stuck. She was a very religious woman," she added at the end, as if that explained it all.

Patience stopped her knitting once again to put her two cents in. "I personally have never liked my name. Have you ever heard of anyone named Patience? People always look at me like 'Okay, what's your real name?' It's very aggravating. I've tried to think of a nickname for myself, like Pat, but Pat seems like *such* a boy's name. I just gave up and let them call me Patience," she said with an irritated shake of her head.

"I think Mother named you Patience because she knew that's what she'd need to raise you all of those years," Nicey said with roll of her eyes. Then she mischievously added, "After all the trouble with you, she named her next one Hope because she was hoping for something better."

"Well, she obviously didn't know what she was doing when she named you, because you're *not* being very nice at the moment," Patience shot back.

Hope just looked at Katherine apologetically.

Katherine excused herself so she could go back to her room before dinner. She didn't want to get in the middle of this discussion. Patience might eat her alive if she said the wrong thing. "Excuse me, ladies, but I was just on my way to my room to rest for a bit before dinner. It was nice to meet you," she said with a smile, as she met all of their eyes except for Patience's, who was determinedly focused on her knitting project.

"So you *are* going to eat out here with us! Feel free to come sit by us at dinner. We'd love to get to know you better," Hope offered cheerfully.

As Katherine closed the door after getting back to her room, she had to stifle a giggle as she thought back to the conversation she just had. This was certainly going to be an interesting place to spend her last years. Not only interesting, but entertaining as well. Despite Patience's brash manner, she decided that she liked all of the sisters. Nicey seemed to be a friendly and almost motherly figure, while Hope seemed very sweet and sincere at the same time. Patience seemed…well, how would one describe her? Unique? Sassy? Crazy? All of the above, Katherine decided.

Katherine wasn't feeling as tired as she had felt earlier, so she sauntered into the bathroom to freshen up a bit. She felt in much better spirits than when she had walked into New Horizons just minutes ago, though she wasn't sure exactly why. As she looked at herself in the mirror, she amusedly assessed her current situation. She mumbled to herself, "I'm 75, I just lost my husband, and I'm living in a place that houses crazy people." Okay, that wasn't really fair. She had only met *one* crazy person. And Patience couldn't really qualify as crazy, just eccentric. On the other hand, she had her health, many years of fond memories with her husband, a roof over her head, and a sense that this was where she was supposed to be at this point in her life. Life is good, she thought as she finished putting on some lipstick and stepped out of the door.

Chapter Five

As Katherine made her way to the commons area, she saw that there were two large tables set up for dinner. Some people were seated at the tables, while others had little folding tables set up in front the easy chairs. The three sisters were still in their easy chairs, with their knitting projects set to the side, and Katherine noticed a fourth chair with a folding table set up in front of it.

Before she had much time to wonder whether or not it was for her, Hope spotted her and waved her over to their little circle. "Katherine, over here! We set up a table for you! It's chicken primavera tonight...yum!"

Katherine smiled. Well, it wasn't too hard to make friends in this place, she mused. "Thanks," she said as she sat down. "I wasn't sure if this seat was for me or if there was a fourth sister I didn't know about," she said with a twinkle in her eyes.

"No, I think Mother had enough on her hands with the three of us," Nicey said with a laugh.

"Speak for yourself! I wasn't any trouble at all!" It seemed that Patience was still trying to redeem herself after Nicey had been teasing her earlier.

"Anyway, I think we should tell you about some of the other residents who live here. You can meet them after dinner," Nicey said in a motherly tone. "The lady with the red hair on the left is named Margaret. Everyone calls her Meg for short. She moved in about a month ago after she was in a car accident that injured her left leg. She didn't want to be a burden to her family, and since she can do pretty much everything for herself, she moved in here."

"Well, she's a burden to me. She's always asking me to get things for her when she's in the commons area, like I'm her housemaid or something. It's not like her leg doesn't work, she just has a little trouble with it is all," Patience mumbled.

"Oh, hush up, Patience. You're going to make Katherine think you're an old grump!" Hope said. She seemed a little embarrassed at times for her sister's antics.

"Ahem, as I was saying," Nicey said, looking at both her sisters. "The gentlemen sitting to the right of Meg is named John. He's only about 65 years old, but his wife died a while back. He moved in two weeks ago."

Katherine winced a little bit at the mention of a spouse dying. She hoped the others didn't notice. She observed that John was still a handsome man and in pretty good shape. He seemed to have a liveliness about him, she could tell, as he spoke to Meg next to him. Katherine noted that he'd be an interesting person to meet later.

"Don't you think he's dreamy?" Hope asked. "He's about my age, and I think he's cute. Don't you, Katherine?"

Before she could say anything, Patience responded for her, "Well, he may be nice to look at, but he flirts with anything that moves. I wouldn't get your hopes up, dear," she said to Hope, who looked a little disheartened at the thought of her crush flirting with others. Then she added, as if it were a fact, "Plus, everyone knows the only reason he moved in here is because he wanted to go out of this world surrounded by a lot of women."

Nicey gasped, "Patience, do you have to have an opinion about everybody? Try to say something nice for once!"

"Well, I would, if there were anything nice to say. I'm just trying to give Katherine some background information that you are leaving out," Patience defended herself, looking at Nicey innocently. Then her face clouded over, "Besides, you know my opinion on men in general."

"Oh yes, you don't need to tell us. 'Men are all pigs. All they're after is a good time and someone to clean up after them.' Does that about sum it up?" Hope asked.

"Yes, but you left out that they're deceptive and smelly," Patience said with her nose in the air.

Katherine got a word in while she had the chance. "Were you never married, then, Patience?"

Patience looked as if she might spit her food out and fall out of her chair. "Married, me? Ha! That would be the day!" She seemed incredulous that Katherine would even entertain such a thought. "Nicey here was married for 45 years…"

"Um, it was 46 years. And you forgot to say 'wonderful years,' thank you very much," Nicey interrupted.

"As I was saying, 46 *wonderful* years," she said the word wonderful very sarcastically, "to a man named Henry."

"He was an amazing man. He died about five years back," she said as she got a little teary-eyed. "Oh, how I do miss that man."

Hope looked at her sister sympathetically. "But you do have the two of us. Don't forget about that!"

Nicey sighed, "Yes, dear, I do have you two. I am so thankful for that. You two have been my saving grace these past few years."

"It's about time you said something nice about me. I was

beginning to feel unappreciated!" Patience said in a mock hurt tone.

Katherine smiled. The sisters were hilarious and heartwarming at the same time. She turned her attention to Hope. "And how about you? Were you ever married, Hope?"

Hope looked down sheepishly. "No, but I was close once."

"Close! You had a boyfriend once, if that's what you mean by close!" Patience corrected. She looked at Katherine, "You see, she has always wanted to be married, but has never found the right person." She softened her tone just a bit, realizing with a glance at her sister that she better be more careful with her words. "We think she's still searching…"

Hope looked a little embarrassed. She tried to explain, "The guy I dated was from high school. I think I always cared for him a little more than he cared about me. I think I scared him away toward the end."

Katherine picked up on her sensitivity on the subject. "But there's always John," she teased with a twinkle in her eyes. Hope blushed, but had a little secretive smile on her face.

"Ahem, well, I don't know how we got so far off the subject. Let's see…who else is there to tell you about?" Nicey scanned the room and proceeded to tell about the other residents seated around the room as they ate their chicken primavera. Patience interrupted about ten times to add in her little tidbits of information about each resident. Each piece of information was entirely factual, of course.

Chapter Six

The three sisters had invited Katherine to bring some sort of a hobby into the commons area after dinner to pass away the evening together. Well, actually, two of the three sisters had invited her. Patience seemed to have the attitude that Katherine might as well come since she had nothing better to do, but she wasn't entirely enthusiastic about the idea. Katherine wasn't going to let that stop her, and plus, she thought, two out of three wasn't bad.

Hope had been wishful that Katherine knitted as well, but Katherine had to admit that she had never done much knitting. Instead, she had told them that she painted quite a bit, and would bring her easel and painting supplies out. Hope had seemed excited about this. "Ooh, a real live artist, here in our very midst!" she had said excitedly.

After retrieving her painting supplies in her room after dinner, Kate arrived to the commons area and stumbled upon the three sisters entrenched deeply into a conversation about something. As usual, Patience was debating her point of view vehemently.

"Well, I realize that you *feel* you had true love with Henry, but I just don't believe that there is such a thing as selfless, love-without-ceasing, give-of-yourself-without-expecting-anything-in-return kind of love. I believe it coming from the woman's side, that she could do that, but I'm not convinced with any of the so-called men who I've met that this kind of love is at all possible. Every man I've met has either ultimately wanted to get a woman into bed with him or to get married so he could have someone to cook and clean up after him."

Hope gasped, "Oh Patience, how can you be so vulgar? Henry wasn't that kind of man! Right, Nicey?"

"No, he most certainly was not," she said emphatically to Patience. "He only ever treated me like a lady, and we never even…" she paused and dropped her voice to a whisper for the next two words, "…*made love* together until after we were married. You know that."

"Well, yes, but he did want someone to cook for him and clean up for him! You can't deny that!" Patience retaliated.

"I cooked meals for him and cleaned up after him because I like to do that kind of stuff. I did it to show that I loved him. He didn't make me do those things."

"And what did he do in return for you? I just don't remember him ever doing that much for you. No offense," Patience prodded.

"Oh, he did a lot of things…he worked all day at a job he didn't entirely like so that he could bring home money for our family. He shoveled, he chopped wood for the woodstove in the winter, and he was a good father to Robert and Douglas. I always knew that he did those things for me as well," Nicey explained thoughtfully.

Patience still didn't seem satisfied with her sister's answer. "Well, I still think that you *feel* it was true love because you were blinded by the marriage bug, but I'm not entirely convinced of it. What I'd like is to hear a story of someone who had a pure, selfless love with a man. I just don't think it will ever happen."

"Well, I don't think you'd recognize true love if it came and bit you in your buttocks!" said a very annoyed Hope.

Patience feigned a hurt look. "Well, now who's being the vulgar one?"

Looking to Katherine as she was setting up her easel, Nicey said, "Maybe Katherine here can help us with our debate. What do you think about it, Katherine?"

"About whether or not there is such a thing as true love?" Katherine inquired. The three sisters nodded. "Well, first of all, let me get this straight. Nicey, you feel as if there is true love because you've had it before." Nicey nodded. "Patience, you feel as if there is no such thing as true love, and never will be."

"Not unless the male genes are altered or lightning strikes," Patience added.

"And, Hope you feel…" Katherine wasn't exactly sure what position Hope was taking.

"I completely believe in true love, but have just never experienced it." She paused and stared wistfully into space. "I'll always be searching for true love, but will probably never find it." As she was staring off into nowhere, John came out of his room and crossed into her line of sight. She looked down and said sheepishly. "Well, maybe I'll find it."

All of the ladies laughed out loud. They knew exactly who and what she was talking about.

Hope turned towards Katherine. "So, what do you think, Katherine? I mean, you know how we all feel now. What do you believe?"

Before Katherine had a chance to answer, Nicey seemed to realize something important, as if she had just remembered something. "Katherine, I just realized that we never asked you if you were ever married during our dinner conversation this evening. Maybe that will have something to do with your answer."

Katherine paused a little awkwardly as all of the three sisters looked at her expectantly. She wasn't sure exactly where to begin. She began slowly, "Well, I think I can answer both the question about being married and about true love in one story. But, I'm afraid it may take a very long time to tell you."

"Oh, do tell! I do love a good story!" Hope said enthusiastically.

"We don't care if it takes a long time. What else do we have to do but knit and gossip?" Nicey added.

"Well, you might as well tell us. It's the only way we're going to get an answer out of you to see if I'm right or not," Patience grumpily agreed.

"Oh, quit being such a party pooper, Patience! Plus, I don't really think there is a right or wrong answer. It's what everyone believes for themselves," Hope chided.

Katherine's eyes lit up as she began to tell her story.

* * * * * * * * *

It was the summer of 1943, and I was just seventeen years old. I had lived here, in Summerville, South Carolina for my whole life. I was an only child, and my parents had been wealthy for as long as I could remember. They had what was called "old Southern money," and it just kept on coming for them. My father did most of his business in Charleston, which wasn't too far away. I was soon to finish high school and attend a finishing school, and my parents were doing all they could to arrange a future marriage with someone from a family equally as wealthy as they were.

* * * * * * * * *

Patience interrupted, "Well, that makes sense to me. If you can't marry for love, you may was well marry for money."

"Quit interrupting! I want to hear the story!" Nicey scolded.

* * * * * * * * *

Anyway, getting married to a wealthy man would have been fine with me at that point in my life, but then a new boy moved into our town. I first saw him at a dance that our town held every summer as part of our summer festivities. I had been scanning the crowd for some of my friends whom I was meeting there, and as my eyes came across him, something made me stop and stare. He was leaning in a sideways sort of way against a building, sipping a Coke and watching the people dance in front of him. He had a calm, confident manner about him, so different from most of the boys I knew. Most of the guys from school would be roughhousing and joking around with each other on the sidelines, hoping to catch some girl's attention, and they definitely wouldn't have the confidence to stand there by themselves. I could see that he was tall and lean with blondish-brown hair and brown eyes. That night, he was wearing a pair of jeans that fit his body well and a green button-up shirt that somehow showed off his toned muscles. I remember thinking to myself, '*Now here's someone I just have to meet.*'

I tried to see if any of my friends knew any information about him, and finally I ran into my friend, Susan. Her boyfriend, George, had already met the new boy earlier that week and had shown him around town a little bit. When I found that out, I almost attacked her with questions about him. By the look on her face, I think she thought I was a little crazy, but I just had to know.

His name was William Brenner. I remember repeating his name slowly after she had said his name, and I liked the way it sounded on my lips. He was a year older than I was in age, but he was to be in the same grade level at school in the fall. Susan said he lived a little outside of town with his dad and two younger siblings, and she had heard they bought the old Mackenzie farm.

"Do you know if he has a girlfriend?" I asked slyly. It wasn't like me to be so forward. I usually kept myself pretty well in line and rarely did anything that would be considered even remotely shocking. My parents had raised me that way.

"Well, aren't we nosy today? If I didn't know any better, I'd think you have a crush on our new boy in town," Susan teased. "You know, Katherine, he's not really your type, though. You usually like the more refined kind of men." She paused for a moment and then said, "He's a country boy, you know."

I mulled that over in my mind. What she said was true. I usually did like the more "refined" kind of men. By that, I know Susan meant the more "wealthy" kind of men, the ones my parents would approve of. For some reason, I did feel an attraction towards him, but I couldn't yet explain why.

Before I had a chance to ask any more questions, Susan's boyfriend George had snuck up behind her and grabbed her around her waist. She squealed as he twirled her around.

"Hey, baby, what's shakin'?" Then he paused and looked at the two of us suspiciously. "What are you two girls up to over here? I feel like I interrupted some important girl talk."

We both just smiled. Susan said, "We were just discussing your new friend, Will."

Will…I liked that. I wondered if that's what everyone called him instead of William.

Susan nodded towards me. "Katherine here was just wondering if you maybe could introduce us to him tonight."

Her eyes twinkled mischievously. "I think she may have a little crush on him."

I swatted at her with my purse. "Oh, come on now! You weren't supposed to say anything! See if I ever tell you anything anymore!" I didn't really care that much, since I thought her saying that might get me an introduction to Will.

"Well, I'm glad she did say something," George bantered, "because my new friend happened to ask who the pretty young woman was with the emerald green eyes across the way."

"He did not!" I gasped. I had a warm sensation wash over me, and I think it went all the way to my face.

"Yes, he did!" George countered. "And by the way you're blushing, I take that to mean you're glad he said that."

I smiled coyly. "Maybe. I'll have to let you know when I actually meet him."

"Well, consider it done," George grabbed Susan's hand with his left and my hand with his right and started to lead us into the direction of where Will was standing.

"What? You mean, right now?" I asked. I wasn't ready. I didn't know what I was going to say. "I wouldn't know what to say to him," I stammered.

George glanced at me a little quizzically. I wasn't usually so shy. "Just be yourself. You seem to get along fine with all the other boys at school. Just pretend he's one of the guys."

Something about him made him seem different than the other boys at school. It wasn't even that I knew he was a country boy or anything else that Susan had told me. He just *seemed* different. Maybe it was in the calm way he was sipping his Coke, just taking it all in without a care in the world. For some reason I just couldn't explain, I felt drawn to him.

As George finished dragging us over to him, I saw Will turn his attention from watching the crowd dance to my eyes. He looked directly at me in a way that seemed to penetrate right through me. He had a slow smile form on his face, and though I think he meant it to silently warm the air in between us, it made my stomach do little flips inside. I couldn't figure out why I felt so nervous. I couldn't even make myself speak. I just stood there staring at him, and then realizing I was doing so, I looked down.

It was a good thing George said something, otherwise we would have just stood there staring at each other all night. I think he sensed my inability to speak, and though I think that he was silently amused by it, he felt like he should help me along a little bit. He said, "William Brenner, this is Katherine Kensington, and Katherine, this is Will."

"Nice to meet you, Will," I managed to say without sounding as nervous as I felt. I suddenly wondered if I should call him Will or William. "Does everyone call you Will? I mean, you don't mind if I call you Will, do you?"

His smile got a little bigger. "Not if someone as pretty as you says it." If any other guy would have said that, I would have thought it was a pick-up line. The way he said it, though, sounded different. It sounded like he didn't just say that to any girl. It sounded...sweet.

I returned his smile. I tried not to blush, though I think I wasn't very successful.

George chuckled a little and clapped his hands together. "Well, I think my work here is done." He then put his arms around the two of us. "You two can stay here and get to know each other better, and I'm going to take my girl over on the dance floor and show all of these people how to dance!" He took Susan's hand and whisked her away into the crowd. She smiled back at me right before George twirled her into his arms dramatically. Good old George.

Will smiled. "George is quite the character."

I laughed. "Yes, he is. Sometimes a little too much the character, I'm afraid."

"Nah, there's no such thing. He's a great guy. He was the first person I met last week, and he offered to show me around. I wasn't expecting to meet people so fast."

"Yeah, if you know George, you know pretty much everybody. He has a way of being friends with everyone he meets." I paused for a second and then asked, "So, what'd you think of our sleepy little town?"

"I like it. I mean, from what I've seen so far." When he said that last part, he looked directly at me, and I knew he was implying me. I felt butterflies all over again.

I looked down and dug my shoe into the dirt a little. I didn't know what to say when he said those kinds of things. I cleared my throat a little. "Where are you from originally? I mean, what made your family move here?"

His face clouded over. It took him a little while to answer. "I used to live on the other side of the state, in a little town outside Greenville. My family had a little farm there. But then, uh..." he paused for a second, "but then, my momma died. My dad didn't want to stay there anymore, so we moved here. I guess my dad used to live here when he was really young, and he thought it'd be a nice place to come back to."

So that was it. I felt horrible about asking. I didn't mean to dig up any painful memories for him. "I'm so sorry about your momma...I bet that was hard." We were both silent for a little bit. He didn't look like he wanted to talk about it anymore, so I changed the subject. "Did your old town used to have dances like this?"

He regained a little smile on his face. "Yeah, we had them once in a while. Usually in the summer, kinda like here. I sometimes used to go with my buddies."

I decided to tease him a little. "Did you used to dance with all of the girls?"

I smiled mischievously.

He teased me right back. "Yeah, they couldn't keep their hands off of me. That's really why I had to move away. I was causing too much of a raucous in town." We both laughed. Then he looked at me a little more seriously. "Actually, I wasn't too interested in any of the girls back home. I've always been busy doing other stuff, and no one really caught my attention as someone who I'd want to be with."

For some reason, I liked the fact that he hadn't really been together with anyone back in his hometown. It made me feel... special. He hadn't come right out and said it or anything, but I felt like he was genuinely interested in me. He had asked George about me, hadn't he? Or had George just made that up to make me feel good? From the way he looked at me, I felt he had to be interested...

He did a little bow and held out his hand. "Miss, would you like to dance?" He looked up expectantly at me.

"I don't dance with strangers," I said, playing a little hard to get.

"Me, neither. That's why I asked you to dance," he said, with a little sparkle in his eye.

* * * * * * * * *

Katherine decided to stop her story there and leave them all hanging in suspense until tomorrow. The clock had just struck 10:00, and that was a lot later than Katherine was used to staying up. She knew it was probably the same for all of these ladies, too. She stifled a yawn. "It's getting late! I guess you will just have to find out the rest tomorrow."

Patience seemed to be the most upset about this. She said,

"What! You mean you're stopping your story there! You're not even going to tell us whether you said 'yes' or not to the dance?"

Nicey and Hope giggled. Nicey said, "I thought you weren't that interested in hearing about 'true love'!"

"I'm not," she snapped. "I just thought it was a good story. Even if it's not one that will convince me about true love."

Nicey and Hope exchanged a knowing look between the two of them. "I guess we'll see…" Hope said teasingly.

"Well, I'm tired anyway. I'm glad she stopped so that we all could get some sleep!" Patience hurriedly put her knitting project in her knitting basket and stomped away to her room.

"Good night, Patience," Nicey said in a sing-song voice to the receding footsteps. There was no answer but a slammed door.

"Do you think she's really mad?" Katherine asked. She didn't want to pick a quarrel with Patience.

Nicey laughed. "No, she'll be fine in the morning. She's just mad at herself because she really wants to hear the story, but she doesn't want anyone to know it. That's just how she is." She gathered her knitting stuff up as well. "Goodnight, my dears. My, I haven't stayed up this late in….well, who knows how long. Goodnight!"

Hope followed closely behind. "Goodnight! I await hearing the rest of your story tomorrow!" She smiled sweetly as she turned to go to her room.

"Goodnight, Nicey. Goodnight, Hope. I'll see you tomorrow." As Katherine began to pick up her painting supplies and easel, she realized with a weary smile that she hadn't painted a thing.

Chapter Seven

Despite the fact that Katherine had gone to bed rather late last evening, she was up with the sunrise to eat an early breakfast and to go on her daily walk. The breakfast in the commons was at 8:00, but she didn't want to wait that long to start her morning. Her father had always been a believer in the idea that 'the early-bird catches the worm,' or as he often said it, 'get up with the sun and you'll get more done.' Her parents had never allowed her to waste her day away being a slug-a-bed, and she was thankful for the habit they had passed down to her. She decided on a bagel with strawberry cream cheese and some fresh fruit before she went out the door.

There were a few people up already when she walked down the hallway past the commons area. She breathed a small sigh of relief when she saw the three sisters were not up yet, as she didn't think she would have been able to sneak past them. It wasn't that she didn't enjoy their company; quite the contrary. She just wanted a little time to herself. John was up reading the paper in one of the easy chairs, and Katherine smiled to herself at Hope's little crush on him. She hoped that perhaps someday the feelings might be returned, or else that Hope would find someone else to share the last part of her life with. She deserved to have a little love in her life. Everyone deserved that chance. Some people were even given a couple of chances, Katherine thought ironically.

As she went out the door, she stopped for a second and looked toward the grove and her old house. She could actually see the roof of her old home poking out from above the hilltop. Her mind drifted to thinking about the new owners. They were a young couple, about 30 years of age, and they were soon to be expecting their first child. Did they like their new home? Would they treasure it, just as Will and Katherine had? She hoped so. The thought suddenly made her feel sad for some reason that she couldn't explain. There were still times that she longed for things to be as they were, with Will and her living each day in good health with an adoring love for each other in their little stone house. Those days were no more.

This is why she needed to walk. The breath of fresh air revitalized her and lifted her spirits. It was a beautiful May morning, with the sun shining and the foliage green around her. She said a little prayer of thanks for her health and the ability to move so freely at her age. In her younger years she would walk four miles a day, but she was grateful for the two miles that she was able to walk now relatively pain-free. She had the occasional stiffness of joints that plagued everyone at her age, but nothing to complain about.

She walked to a nearby park that she had frequented on her walks many a times in the past. It was less than a mile from New Horizons, and she figured she could loop around on some of the paths in a northeasterly direction so that she would eventually end up near the grove. That would be a good ending place each morning…a place where she could sit on her bench to collect her thoughts and visit Will.

Katherine walked at a brisk pace and started to break a sweat after a half a mile. Some days she went at more of a leisurely pace, but today she felt like pushing herself a little. The birds were out, hopping around in the sunshine looking for food. Katherine had always loved the birds. She and Will had always had a variety of bird feeders out in their yard, and she felt that one of the simplest pleasures in life was watching the birds flutter in and out of the trees, singing to each other in their chipper voices. When she had moved into New Horizons, she was happy to see that there were multiple bird feeders placed around the property. There was even a bird feeder right outside one of her windows, and she was glad she would be able to watch her little friends in the future.

Before she knew it, Katherine had already walked through the park trails and was approaching the grove. She slowed her pace a bit as she neared the trees, her feet eventually finding the well-worn path that led to the clearing. She slowly came from around the back of the gravestone and sat on the bench. The sun flitted through the trees, illuminating much of the bench and the gravestone. She sat for a few moments, not saying anything, then deciding to voice some of her thoughts out loud.

She took a deep breath and sighed. "I didn't write any poems for you today, so I'm just going to tell you what's on my mind." She paused for a second, her face forming into a smile. "I met a few friends yesterday at New Horizons…three, actually. They're sisters, and hilarious ones at that. I spent all last evening with them, and I'm sure that I'll be spending a good portion of each day with them as well. The oldest is named Nicey, the middle sister Patience, and the youngest one Hope. Patience is a real spitfire. I can't tell if she likes me or not. I think she does, but she doesn't want anyone to know it." Her smile widened a bit. "I've been telling them our story…but I haven't gotten very far yet. I'm only on the part where I met you at the town dance."

Her eyes looked up wistfully into the trees. "Remember that, Will? Remember how I was so nervous to talk to you, and you kept saying things that would make me look down and blush? I'd never had a guy who made me nervous before."

She stared at the gravestone, momentarily lost in her reminisce, and then collected her thoughts once again. "Anyway, talking about us made me remember so many things…things that I perhaps haven't told anyone before. There's so much I haven't told them yet…I think they're going to be really surprised by the end of the whole story. I know that I was in real life. I still am surprised that you…" She paused, looking for the right words. "I still am surprised that you loved me through the whole mess I made of my life. I can't believe you waited for me."

Katherine got a little teary-eyed and looked down, deep in thought. Her fingers ran over the inscription carved on the front side of the bench. Like a blind woman reading Braille, she slowly let her fingers feel every letter of the simple phrase "Will loves Katherine," as she had done a hundred times over.

Will had made the bench for Katherine as a surprise shortly after they had gotten married and purchased the property so many years ago. He hand-made it out of cedar, and his finishing touch had been the inscription on the front. She remembered the morning that he had blindfolded her and led her down the path to the clearing. Giggling like a schoolgirl, Katherine had been peppering Will with questions as to what the surprise could be. She knew that he had been working on something, since he had spent multiple hours toiling away in the workshop that week. Any time Katherine had asked what he was up to, he had simply said, "You'll see," with a mysterious smile and a twinkle in his eyes.

The bench had been a wonderful surprise, but even more wonderful was where he had put it. It was in their clearing; the very place that Will had come back to her and asked her to be his wife. This was why Katherine could never sell the grove. All of her happiest memories could be traced to this very place. And, as Katherine observed as she looked down at the gravestone, her saddest memories as well.

She gradually stood up and walked over to the gravestone. She kissed her hand and placed it on Will's name. "Katherine loves Will, too," she said quietly as she slowly made her way back down the path from where she had come.

* * * * * * * * *

Patience was looking out the big bay window toward the front of New Horizons a few hours after breakfast was over. "Where is she?" she wondered aloud to nobody in particular. "She's been gone for hours."

Nicey overheard her and smiled at Hope. "It appears that our sister, who seemingly didn't want anything to do with our friend or her story, can't wait for her to get back. How interesting..."

Patience whipped around. "I heard that!" she said grumpily. "I'll have you know that the only reason I want her to get back is so that I can hear the rest of her story. You two know that I've always liked a good story, and I want to hear how this one turns out," she said snippily. Then she added, "Not that it will change my mind about true love. So don't get any ideas!" She turned her head back to looking at the window as her two sisters quietly giggled over their knitting projects.

Patience was looking at some of the birds on the birdfeeders outside when she spotted something moving in the distance that caught her attention. She adjusted her glasses a little and saw that it was a someone, not a something. The person came out of a grove of trees about a half a mile ahead and was walking straight toward New Horizons. As the figure came closer into view, she thought it looked a bit like Katherine. Sure enough, as the figure walked across the street, Patience discovered she was right. She looked over at Nicey and Hope to see if they had seen Katherine as well, but they were busy working on their knitting projects and chatting. *'Hmmm…,'* thought Patience, *'I'll just have to figure out what she was doing in that grove of trees over there. I swear that's private property. Ohhh…I won't have a moment's peace until I figure this all out!'*

Patience quickly walked over to one of the easy chairs to settle in with her knitting project so that she looked as if she had been there all morning. Nicey noticed her brisk pace over to the chair and how she hurriedly got her knitting project out. She looked curiously at her sister, cocking one eyebrow. She was up to something.

Katherine stepped into the doorway and looked around the commons area. Her eyes needed to adjust from being outside in the sun for the past hour. As she focused a little, she saw the three sisters nestled in the chairs working on their knitting projects. By the looks of it, they had been there all morning. If she had looked a bit more closely, she would have noticed that Patience's project hadn't progressed since last evening.

"Hi, ladies. I see you're up and hard at work already," she said as she sat down into the unoccupied easy chair.

"Well, some of us have been hard at work, at least," Nicey said, looking pointedly at Patience.

Patience acted like she had no idea what her sister was talking about. She decided to ask Katherine some questions before she had a chance to notice anything. "Yes, we are hard at work, as usual. So…where did you go to this morning? You look as if you have been walking."

"Oh yes, I have. I go on a walk every morning. I always feel so much better when I've had a little exercise to start my day. You ladies should try it sometime."

Hope looked interested. "How far do you walk each day?" she asked.

"About two miles. I used to do more, but these old joints just can't handle it. My mind is willing, but my body is weak," she joked.

"Tell me about it," Nicey said. She had pretty bad arthritis at times, and took daily medication for it. For the time being, she could still knit, but it might not be long until she'd have to be content to just sit and visit.

Patience didn't like the direction this conversation was going. She reiterated, "Yes, but *where* do you go walking? Anywhere special around here?"

Nicey noticed the innocent sound to Patience's questioning. What was she getting at? She was *definitely* up to something.

"Oh, here and there. I walked over to the park just under a mile from here. I walked a loop around some of the paths and then headed back," she said vaguely.

'*She's hiding something*,' Patience thought to herself. She'd have to ask more questions later.

Hope seemed not to have caught on to any of this. "Well, we can't wait to hear the rest of your story." She looked over at Patience and smiled mischievously. "Especially Patience over here."

"Well, she did kind of leave us hanging the other night," Patience said in her own defense. Then she mumbled, "What kind of person leaves a story in a place like that, anyway?"

They all laughed. Katherine said, "Well, lunch is in just a little while. I thought I'd go back to my room for a bit to get ready for the day and organize some of my stuff from moving in. Then I'll tell you more after lunch. How does that sound?" She looked around at them. They were all nodding except for Patience.

"Fine by me. I can wait," Patience said smugly, her eyes glued to her knitting.

"Well, I'll see you ladies at lunch, then." She was going to leave it at that, but just couldn't resist adding, "Happy knitting, Patience!"

All Katherine got as a reply was a slight glare from the top of Patience's glasses as she made her way back to her room.

CHAPTER EIGHT

AFTER A TASTY lunch of pesto pasta, salad, and fresh fruit, the four ladies settled down with their afternoon activities. The three sisters were, of course, knitting, while Katherine had brought in some letters to write to a few friends who had moved away. She knew from last night's experience that trying to paint something was hopeless, but she thought she could squeeze in a few letters in the afternoon somehow.

Though nothing had been said aloud, Nicey, Hope, and Katherine had all made up their minds not to say anything about continuing the story until Patience did. They knew that it would eventually drive her crazy, but that was the fun in it.

They all sat quietly for about 20 minutes, with Katherine almost completing an entire letter, when Patience burst out, "Okay, okay, you guys win. Tell us the rest of the story already!"

The other three burst out laughing. It was so fun to tease her sometimes.

"Let's see...I was at the part where Will had asked me to dance..."

* * * * * * * * *

I did, of course, say yes. And boy, did we dance. We danced all night. He was a pretty good dancer. In fact, he was the best dancing partner I'd ever had.

After dancing to a few songs, I asked, "And where did you learn to dance, Mr. Brenner? You're pretty good for a country boy."

He cocked one eyebrow at me. "And how, may I ask, did you know I was a country boy?"

Oops. I had given myself away. Now he knew that I had been asking around about him. I tried to come up with a good excuse. "Well, you did say you lived on a farm before you moved here," I explained. He didn't look like he believed me. "Or, I may have asked Susan about you, and she just might have told me," I said mysteriously.

"Well, I asked about you, too. But I'm sure George told you that," he said with a wink. He went on, "When I was about eight years old, I was going to my first town dance with my parents. I just wanted to hang out with my buddies, but my momma was convinced that I should know how to dance with a girl in case I saw one I thought was pretty. I remember her putting on some music and grabbing my hand, and I kept saying, 'Aww, momma, do I have to learn this stuff?' She just smiled and kept telling me that I'd be thanking her some day for teaching me to dance."

"Well, did you ever get a chance to use your new talent at the dance?" I asked him, curious to know about the eight-year-old Will Brenner.

"I almost got away with not having to use it, but then my momma stepped in. She called me over to her and pointed out a pretty little girl standing on the side watching people dance. I told her I wasn't interested in girls, but she all but made me go over there and ask her to dance anyway. She said, 'Will, honey, do it for your momma.' I felt like I couldn't disrespect her, and she did have an awful lot of pride in the fact that she taught me to dance, so I went over and asked her. All my buddies were on the side laughing at me. I think they secretly wanted to know how to dance, too, but they'd never admit it. Anyway, I danced a whole song with Fanny Mae Bailey in front of everyone."

I laughed. "So, you still remember her name, huh? She must have made quite the impression on you," I teased.

"Well, matter of fact, she did. Only because the whole crowd of people stopped and clapped for us at the end of the song. I was the center of attention." He smiled mischievously, "And because her name was Fanny. Being eight years old, that is one hilarious name for a girl." He giggled like he was eight years old again.

I swatted at him, "Well, aren't you terrible! Here, I thought you were so mature and all. I guess I was deceived." I smiled playfully at him.

An apologetic smile formed on his face. He placed his hand on the small of my back and slowly brought me towards him as the next song started. It was a slow one, the first slow one they had played since we started dancing. Looking right into my eyes, he said, "I would never deceive you, Katherine Kensington. Never in a million years." Then he dipped me dramatically, and as my head came back up, my eyes found his. This time, I didn't look away.

We danced until our feet were sore, talking in between the dances, getting to know each other on that warm summer night. I felt as if we were the only two on the dance floor, and when he looked at me with that penetrating gaze of his, I felt as if I were the only girl he wanted to be with. Those brown eyes of his... they seemed to see right through me to my very soul. I'd never had a guy look at me that way before. Most guys would look at me appreciatively, admiring the outward beauty that I'd been told I had, but their gaze never seemed to see the real me.

It was then that I realized that my life might not go according to the plan my parents had made for me. William Brenner had just thrown a hitch in that plan.

* * * * * * * * *

"Well, I'll say he threw a hitch in your parents' plan!" Nicey said somewhat dramatically after I had paused for a bit in my story.

"Oh, how romantic!" Hope exclaimed. "Imagine, meeting him and dancing with him all night! I wish it had been me!"

"Well, it wasn't!" Patience chimed in. "And you two are interrupting the story when it's just about to get good!" She turned and looked at Katherine. "Well, what happened next? Did he kiss you? Are there any other juicy details!"

Hope gasped. "Patience, you really are a little devil. This isn't a smut story!"

Patience looked hurt. "I know that. I just wanted to hear what happened next."

Nicey chimed in. "I think we all do. Sorry for interrupting. Go on Katherine, get on with the 'juicy details,' as Patience put it," she said as she smiled at Patience to put her at ease. "You were talking about the hitch in the plan," she prodded.

"Yes, and no more interruptions!" declared Patience.

* * * * * * * * *

Will definitely changed life in the Kensington family. After the dance, Will and I were inseparable. Most of the time, we went out with George and Susan. The four of us would always find something fun to do, whether it be going to the movies or to the town fair, or if it were nice out, swimming in the local swimming holes. After Will and George were done with their work for the day, we would spend every waking moment together.

I hadn't really told my parents about Will, since I knew they wouldn't approve. I knew they were beginning to get suspicious, since I had been going to "visit Susan" virtually every night since the dance.

One night, a few weeks after the dance, my mother started questioning me. At dinner, she said, "Katherine, dear, it seems that you've been seeing a lot of Susan lately. What have you two been up to?" The way she said it, I knew that she suspected something. I thought I'd try to be evasive as long as possible without technically lying.

"Well, we've been going to the movies and spending time at the town fair. It's been such a nice summer, and we don't want to waste the days away doing nothing," I said, hoping that would be enough to appease her. It wasn't.

"Has there been anyone else with whom you've been spending time?" she questioned. Her eyes looked directly at me. I knew I couldn't get out of this one without telling her a lie, so I figured now was as good of a time as any to tell her the truth.

My eyes averted her direct stare while I gathered up my courage. "Well, actually, there is someone whom I met at the dance a few weeks ago who has been coming along as well." I paused, trying to figure out exactly what I wanted to say. "George and Susan introduced me to him. He's a new boy in town, and he's going to be going into my grade this fall at school. His name is Will, and we've become good friends. I think that you'd really like him." My last statement was more of a wishful one than a true one, but I thought by saying it that I might convince them as well as myself.

My father piped in. "A new boy, you said? The only new

people who have moved into town who I know of is that farming family…Brenner, I believe the name is." His brow furrowed, obviously perplexed by the mystery. "It couldn't be him…so, who is it?"

This is the part of the conversation that I had been dreading. I knew that my parents wouldn't approve of a farmer, unless he was a very wealthy farmer…no matter how nice he was. I cleared my throat, hoping to sound confident before my father. "Daddy, actually, it is the family you spoke of. William Brenner is his full name." I felt the need to explain further, as if saying more about him might convince my parents to have an open mind. "His family does farm, but Will has great ambitions for his future. He may not have a lot of money right now, but I know that he is talented and has the ability to make something of himself."

I looked at my parents' faces. They looked a little shocked at this new information, and definitely not convinced by what I said, but for some reason not apparent to me at the time, neither one commented any further on him. My father looked at me and simply said, "Why don't you bring him by tomorrow for dinner so that we can meet him properly. I'd like to meet this young man and find out more about him for myself."

"Yes, we'll have something delicious prepared for dinner, and you bring William on over. Then we can all have a nice chat," my mother chimed in.

They were being strangely pleasant about all of this. I knew that I shouldn't get my hopes up at this point, though. They may be open to having him over for dinner, but I knew that dinner was not going to be a casual occasion. It would be a time for my father to grill Will with questions that he might be uncomfortable in answering. No, I wasn't looking forward to this dinner. Not at all.

It was strange to me that just a couple of weeks ago I would have abhorred at the thought of even dating a farmer. Here I was entertaining the thought of a future with one, and trying to convince my parents to entertain that thought as well. At this point, though, my parents had no idea how very deeply I already cared about Will. I don't even know if I had an idea.

* * * * * * * * *

"What happened to the first kiss?" Patience asked rather impatiently. "You must have skipped that part!"

"Well, look who's interrupting now!" Nicey exclaimed. "I thought that you were the one who wanted her to 'continue her story without any interruptions.'"

Katherine thought this might be a good time to intervene. "Actually, I haven't gotten to that part yet," she explained. "Remember, it was only 1943. Girls didn't go around kissing boys on the first date like they do nowadays. Plus, Will really was a gentleman. He didn't want to do anything to make me feel uncomfortable. And, at this point, we had only known each other for a few weeks." Katherine looked over in time to catch the disappointed look on Patience's face. Hoping to appease her, she added, "Don't worry, Patience, the first kiss is coming up soon. Just be patient!"

Nicey smiled. "I think that's a little contrary to her nature. You better tell about it quickly, or you may lose an audience member," she said with a pointed glance at her sister.

"Ohhh, yes, let's hear about the kiss!" Hope said with a little clap of her hands. She had been waiting for that part in the story as well.

* * * * * * * * *

After dinner that night, I excused myself and called Will from our phone in the study, which was the only really private place there was to talk in the house. I told him about how my parents wanted to have him over for dinner the next evening.

"Really? That's a good sign, isn't it? I've been wanting to meet your parents for a while, anyway. I mean, you've met my dad and everything already," Will said expectantly.

It was true I had met his father multiple times in the short few weeks that we had known each other. His father was a simple man. Not as in simple-minded…he just lived a simple lifestyle. I almost envied it. He was the kind of man who lived life for faith, family, and friends, and in that order. My parents were always bustling about with social obligations that were attended merely for show and social advancement. I loved my parents dearly, but there seemed to be an emptiness in the way and in the reason they lived their lives compared to Will's family. I just couldn't explain it.

Will's father was tall and lean, just like Will, with a tanned body from working long hours out in the sun. I could see that he had passed his kind, brown eyes down to his son, and I could also sense the bond the two had with each other. After I had met his father for the first time, Will had explained to me that their bond was from working together on the farm all of his years growing up. He had also mentioned how his mother's death had brought them even closer together as a family. I could sense the heaviness that plagued Will still about his mother's death as he spoke of it.

Will's father had accepted me the moment I stepped into his door, and he had even teased me a little for good measure. Will told me beforehand that he teased everyone, and the best way to handle him was to tease him back. And that's exactly what I did. He seemed impressed by my wit, and we took to bantering back and forth every time we saw each other. Will seemed to enjoy the exchanges we had. He had later told me that his father liked me and wanted me to stick around.

I thought of all of this now as I tried to think of what to say to Will. My parents' invitation to have him over for dinner wasn't made with the same intentions as his father's invitations to stop over. My father intended to interrogate him and intimidate Will into not dating me at all. I knew that Will cared too much about me to let himself be intimidated, but I was still scared of what the dinner would hold.

I cleared my throat. "Will, I don't know how to say this, but I don't want you to get your hopes up. It might not be such a good sign. My parents aren't like yours. When it comes to my future, my parents care only about money and their social position. They're not bad people, they're just…different. To be honest, I think my dad is going to try to scare you away. He might not, but that's what I think he will do." I heaved a worried sigh on my side of the phone.

"Why do you think that, Kate? He doesn't even know me." Will had called me Kate almost from the get-go. No one else called me this, and I liked the way it sounded rolling off of his tongue. It made me feel special to have my own name from him.

"Well…" I searched for the right words. "My father is a person who is used to getting what he wants in life. He comes from a family of old Southern money, and he has always been given what he wants when he wants it. He, well, to be precise, both of my parents, have a kind of ideal person in mind for me. When I say 'ideal', I mean one who is just like my father and fits into their grand scheme for the Kensington family's future. They, of course, want someone who will love me and take good care of me. The problem is this person would also have to fit into their little social circle and already be well-off financially." I paused briefly to take some of the sting off of my next statement. "Their ideal person for me is…not you."

CHAPTER NINE

Nicey gasped when Katherine said the last statement. "How did he react when you said *that*?" She had a look of disbelief on her face that seemed to say that she thought Katherine perhaps had been a little too blunt with Will.

Katherine smiled a wistful little smile remembering his reaction. "Will was always the eternal optimist. He said that I must be exaggerating and that we should just wait to see what happened. He reassured me that no matter how my father acted at dinner the following night, his feelings for me wouldn't change."

Hope smiled. "I love optimists. I always try to be an optimist. The world looks much brighter that way."

Patience's brow furrowed and her eyes clouded over. "I'd never want to be an optimist. It seems like all that happens is you get your hopes up and then it all comes crashing down on you. It's better not to hope for anything good and then be surprised if something good does happen."

"Maybe, but I'd rather think good things are going to happen to me and be disappointed than think bad things were going to happen and be right," Hope responded.

Nicey added, "And I'd rather be someone who was pleasant to be around than an old grouch who thinks the sky will fall at any moment!"

Patience seemed genuinely offended. "I'm not a grouch, I'm just a realist. They're two entirely different things." She got a smug look on her face and continued, "You all need a dose of reality once in a while. It's a good thing I'm around, or you two would float away with all of the false optimistic thoughts ballooning in your heads!"

Just as Nicey had steeled herself to respond, the dinner bell sounded to warn the residents that dinner would be served in a half an hour. It couldn't have come at a better time, Katherine mused. The three sisters seemed as if they were headed into a heated debate. The clanging of the bell seemed to cut through at least *some* of the tension in the room.

"Saved by the bell, it seems," Nicey decided to say instead of what she seemed intent on saying beforehand. She sighed. "I need to go to my room for a bit before dinner. I might try to get a little cat-nap in before we eat. Speaking of cats, I miss my little Fluffy. They don't allow people to bring pets here, so I had to give him away before I moved in. I hope he's doing well."

"Your *little* Fluffy?" Patience said sarcastically. "That thing was a big fat oaf, and about as dumb as one, too! I'm glad they don't allow pets in here. That thing used to try to bite me every time I came over to your place."

"You were the only one he ever tried to bite!" Nicey replied. Then she got a little smile on her face as she said the next bit. "Hmmm…I wonder why?"

"I never did anything to him! I just tried to pet him and give him treats once in a while. No harm in that!" Patience retorted.

"I don't think rat poison constitutes as a cat treat," Nicey said with a twinkle in her eye. "Don't think I didn't know you were the one who put it there. It's a good thing my Fluffy was so smart that he didn't even eat the poison."

Patience got an innocent look on her face and started knitting at a ferocious pace. "I have no idea what you're talking about."

Katherine supposed this was as good as a time as any to sneak away to her room before dinner. Hope spotted her as she was halfway to her door.

"Katherine, you never got to the part about the kiss! When will we hear about that?" she asked expectantly.

Her question snapped Patience and Nicey out of their argument about Fluffy. Patience said, "I was wondering where the kiss went, too. I hope you didn't lead Will on as badly as you're leading us on, or he might have died from old age before he ever got a kiss out of you!"

Katherine couldn't help but let a giggle out. These three sisters were something else. "I'll get to that part after dinner." After seeing Patience's skepticism written all over her face, she added, "You will hear about the kiss before the night is over. I *promise.*"

"Well, it's about time…" Patience mumbled as Katherine slipped into her room.

Once back into her room, Katherine sat down on the edge of the bed, leaned back, and closed her eyes. It was a bit tiring telling this story. She wanted to do the tale justice and not leave anything out. The problem was that in telling the story, it forced Katherine to rehash her past, which was a difficult task considering some of the poor decisions she had made…decisions she would have given anything to undo. It also made Katherine painfully aware of how much she loved Will and how much she had lost when he died. The story needed to be told, if not for the sake of the three sisters, for her own sake, Katherine thought as she let her muscles relax into the comfort of her bed.

Katherine awakened with a start about 25 minutes later. She looked at her clock and realized that she must have fallen asleep. Frustrated with herself, she realized that she was a few minutes late for dinner. "I really am getting old," she muttered to herself as she hastily put on her sweater. "Next thing you know I'll miss dinner completely. Wouldn't the three sisters be getting impatient to hear the rest of the story if that happened!" she chuckled to herself as she stepped out of her door.

As she came into the lobby, Katherine took a seat in the easy chair that had come to be accepted as "Katherine's chair" by the three sisters and all of the other residents of New Horizons. Patience gave her a mischievous smile as Katherine placed her napkin in her lap. Katherine couldn't help but wonder what that smile meant. "What is that smile for?" she asked.

"Oh, nothing." After a pause, she said, "I just think that you and Nicey both went to the same place before dinner and were attacked by the sheet fairies!"

Katherine looked blankly at Nicey and then back again at Patience.

Hope intervened. "What she means is that you both have sheet lines on your faces from taking naps," she said with a smile.

Katherine got out of her chair and looked in one of the lobby mirrors. Sure enough, there was a big line across her cheek. She looked down at Nicey to see an identical line on her face. All four of the ladies giggled. "I guess I fell asleep for a little while," Katherine admitted sheepishly.

"It happens to the best of us," Nicey said. "I had a nice little nap and dreamed of Henry and Fluffy," she said with a content smile on her face. "They were both alive and well, and then I woke up here. I was a little confused at first, and then realized where I was. I guess I still wish things were the way they used to be once in a while," Nicey said with a little regret in her voice.

Katherine gave her an empathetic smile. "I know exactly what you mean, Nicey. I feel the exact same way sometimes."

"What, you two aren't happy living here with Hope and my charming self?" Patience asked with mock hurt in her voice.

"Yes, good thing you are so charming or I would miss Henry a lot more," Nicey quipped. All the ladies laughed except for Patience.

Before Patience could respond, Hope turned her attention to Katherine as she was getting her tray of food adjusted. "We just can't wait to hear more about the dinner party and your first kiss!" Hope said.

Katherine smiled. "Well, I was going to save the story until after dinner, but I guess I could tell it while we eat. I mean, it is entirely appropriate since it is a dinner story and we happen to be eating dinner."

"Maybe it'll feel like you're really there again," Nicey prodded.

"Trust me, I wouldn't *want* to be there again. I'm afraid it ended up worse than I had ever imagined it," Katherine said sadly.

* * * * * * * * *

That evening, I nervously awaited Will's arrival out on our veranda, alternating between sitting and standing as I looked toward the gate that was the entrance to our property. Earlier, I had been waiting in the living room with my mother, trying to strike up a conversation with her to cut through the tension that was in the air, but the sight of her made me too nervous and I soon had ventured outside. I knew that my mother could be just as intimidating as my father when she wanted to be, and I hoped that she would be merciful tonight.

Dinner was to be served at 6:00 sharp. I had told Will to be a little early since my parents highly approved of punctuality, and he promised he would arrive "with time to spare." He had also said to quit worrying. I wish I could have been as calm and confident as he was, but then again, he didn't know my parents. Soon enough, I saw the gates open and Will walking through them towards me. His family did own a car, but it was a nice evening and he must have decided to walk.

I watched as he leisurely walked up the long driveway and onto the veranda steps, looking as if he didn't have a care in the world. I must have been holding my breath because I exhaled loudly as soon as he was close to me.

Will laughed. "What, were you afraid I wouldn't come?"

I looked down sheepishly as I nervously wrung my fingers. "No, I was more afraid of what would happen *after* you came," I said honestly.

He put his hand under my chin and tipped my head up, looking directly into my eyes. "Kate, you don't need to worry. There's no way your parents could scare me away from you. I know we've only known each other for a few short weeks, but my feelings for you are…" he paused, searching for the words, "…are like nothing I've ever felt for any girl before. It's not something I'm going to just walk away from without a fight."

I didn't know what to say. I'd felt drawn to him since the first moment I saw him at the dance for reason I couldn't explain. The past two weeks had only strengthened my feelings for him, which went against everything my head told me was right. He was so different from the ideal my parents had formed for me, yet, when I pictured my ideal, only Will came to mind. I wanted all of him: his unwavering faith, his love of what is good and true in this world, and his simple view of life. From the very beginning, it was as if he had the ability to see into my very being. He saw the real me.

Just as I was about to respond, my father came out the front door. He took note of Will's hands holding mine and coughed loudly. He stuck out his hand, more so as a way to get Will's hands off mine than as a friendly gesture. "You must be William. My daughter has told me quite a bit about you. I look forward to observing the many qualities I am told you possess." He said the last part a bit skeptically, as if there was no way that Will would ever measure up to what I had told them. I suspected that even if he did, he still wouldn't be good enough for my parents.

If Will had noticed the doubtful inflection in my father's voice, he wasn't showing it. He shook my father's hand confidently. "Sir, I look forward to getting to know you and your wife better, although I hope Kate here hasn't embellished me so much that I won't be able to meet her standards." He looked at me with a slightly reproachful look combined with a somewhat amused grin.

My father looked straight at Will. "I wouldn't worry too much about that. I don't think 'Kate' has set the standard too high at all."

Although my father's reply could have been taken two different ways, Will and I both knew what he meant by it. There was an awkward silence to follow.

My father smiled as if nothing had happened. "Let's head inside and have some supper. You know how your mother hates it if people are late." He walked in the front door without giving us time to respond.

Will and I looked at each other. If that was only the beginning, it was surely going to be a long evening.

* * * * * * * * *

Nicey huffed in an agitated manner and interrupted Katherine's story. "Well, I can't believe your father said that when he had just met Will. He didn't even give him a fair chance!"

Hope looked as if she might cry. "How horrible! I would have just wanted to crawl under a rock and die!"

Patience looked annoyed that her sisters had interrupted the story once again. "Well, how would that have helped anything? Anyway, maybe Katherine misinterpreted what her father meant. Maybe he just meant that he thought Will didn't need worry about disappointing them if Will didn't exactly match up to what Katherine had told them. Maybe he was just trying to be nice."

Nicey and Hope gave Katherine an apologetic look. Katherine said, "If only that were true. Based on the rest of the evening, I'm pretty sure he meant something else."

"Well, let's hear what happened anyway. We know that first kiss is coming up sometime soon!" Hope prodded.

"Yes, let's get on to that before I fall asleep waiting for it!" Patience said with a yawn.

Katherine laughed as she looked at her watch. "Sorry, it is getting kind of late. I'll try to shorten the dinner story a bit so I can get to the first kiss. I *did* promise I would get to that tonight, after all," she said as she looked at Patience.

* * * * * * * *

Leaving the safety of the veranda, Will and I made our way to the dining room. My mother and father were standing by their chairs, waiting for us to enter and be seated. As we all sat down and the dining room staff brought in the first course, my father turned his attention towards Will. Though his voice sounded pleasant and conversational, I feared the questions would be anything but that.

"So, William...what brought you and your family to our sleepy little town?"

I tried to catch my father's eye. I had specifically asked him not to ask any questions that would lead Will to have to talk about his mother's death. He could only be doing this for one reason: to make Will uncomfortable. He avoided my eyes and kept his penetrating gaze focused on Will.

Will cleared his throat and took a moment to consider what he wanted to say. "Well, sir, my family just needed a little change of pace. You see, my parents owned a farm right outside of Greenville for as long as I could remember. Then, about a year ago, my momma got pretty sick." He paused for a second, looking at me before continuing. "She passed away this past spring. I guess it was too hard on my dad to stay in our house, since everything reminded him of her. My dad used to live here when he was younger, so he decided that it was as good a place as any to start over." He smiled at me as he continued. "So far, it seems like it has worked out all right for us."

I smiled back at Will, holding his gaze so that he wouldn't have to look at my father's formidable face.

My father saw the exchange and cleared his throat, diverting Will's attention away from me and back to him. He didn't seem too pleased with the direction of this conversation. "Well, I'm sure it will take time before you'll be able to assess whether or not it has worked out in your best interest. Time does have a way of changing things."

I'm pretty sure what my father meant was that *he* had a way of ensuring that things would change according to his plan with the passing of time. Will must have sensed this as well, but he stood his ground.

Will met my father's gaze as he spoke. "I happen to agree

with you, sir. My dad has always said that he thinks things often get sweeter with time. I'm hoping that will be true of our family's move here."

My father seemed to sense the challenge in his voice and rose to meet it. "We'll just have to see what the future holds for you. You never can tell what will happen, can you?"

Maybe I was reading into things, but there seemed to be a hint of a threat in my father's last statement.

My mother, sensing the tension in the room, attempted to lighten the mood. "Is anyone up for dessert? The cook has prepared a delicious peach cobbler."

As we all murmured in agreement about dessert, I shot my mom a thankful look. Even though I know she sided with my father on this one, she had decided to show some compassion on my plight tonight.

With that, we finished the rest of the dinner in silence. Afterwards, as the dinner staff was clearing the table, I asked my parents if we could be excused. Will thanked my parents for dinner, and we walked back out to the veranda.

As soon as we were out of hearing distance, I turned to Will. "I am *so* sorry about my father. I told you he could be a bear sometimes." I gave him an apologetic look.

Will started to chuckle. "Well, in all fairness, you *did* warn me. He was a little…protective of you." He seemed as if he wanted to use a different word instead of protective, but thought better of it.

I gave him a skeptical look. "Protective? I'm not sure if that would be the word that I'd use for it."

He smiled sheepishly. "I was going to say overbearing and intimidating, but went with protective instead." He paused for a second and then said, "Although, if I were him and had a daughter like you, I would be a little protective, too."

I rolled my eyes. "Gee, thanks. I'm pretty sure I can take care of myself...without the protection of *either* of you."

He gave me a mock hurt look. "Hey now, don't get all high and mighty on me. I was just saying *if* I were him." He sighed and then took on a little more of a serious tone. "And I'm definitely not anything like him. Just ask him and he'll tell you."

Sensing his frustration, I smiled at him. "I know, and I'm glad you're not like him." I paused thoughtfully. "You know, I used to think I wanted to be with someone just like my daddy. And then I met you."

Giving me a thankful look, he reached for my hands and interlaced his fingers in mine. He cleared his throat and said, "Do you think your parents would let you go for a walk with me? There's a spot a little less than a mile from here that I'd like to take you."

I raised my eyebrows curiously. "And where might that be? I like to know where I'm headed before I agree."

"Oh, you'll see. I reserve the right to keep that to myself for now. Just tell your parents that you will be walking in a northwesterly direction," he said with a mischievous twinkle in his eye.

I couldn't help but laugh. "I'm sure *that* will go over well, considering how well the evening has gone so far." Nonetheless, I went inside and asked my parents.

When I came back out, Will was looking at me expectantly. "Well...?"

I smiled at him. "It took a little convincing, but they said yes. We only have an hour, so we'll have to walk fast. We have to be back by 8:00 sharp."

He gave me a little salute. "Yes, ma'am!" He grabbed my hand and took off at a brisk pace.

I started giggling as I practically had to run to keep up with him. "I didn't mean *that* fast. I'll be so out of breath I won't be able to say anything!"

He slowed his pace and smiled at me. "I know. I just wanted you to know that I am a man of my word. I *will* have you back by 8:00, even if I have to carry you back."

We talked very little as we walked, just happy to be in each other's company. That's one thing I loved about Will. He was comfortable with silence as much as he was with conversation.

We soon came to the end of the road. I gave Will a perplexed look. He answered my unspoken question by leading me through some taller grass that gracefully tickled my free hand as we went deeper into the field.

I could contain my curiosity no longer. "Will, where are we going? You can't keep me in suspense forever!"

He looked back at me and smiled amusedly. "We are almost there. Just a few minutes more…"

True to his word, we soon came to a grove of trees in the middle of the field. He led me through a myriad of trees and into a little clearing. As we stopped and Will guided my eyes upward, I couldn't help but gape at the beauty that surrounded us. The trees, a mixture of oak, poplar, and pine, almost seemed to arch over the clearing, making it seem like a little room apart from the rest of the world. Soft pine needles fallen from years past made a perfect layer of bedding for my feet as I turned around in circles, taking it all in. I had a hard time forming words as I tried to ask Will about it. "How…Where…When did you find this place?" I finally stammered.

"My house is just a few miles northwest of here, at least as the crow flies. I took a shortcut to get to your house tonight, and I ended up walking through here. I felt compelled to stop. I sat on one of the fallen trees for a few minutes, taking it all in as you just did. I would have stayed here longer, but *someone* told me to be early for dinner." He looked at me pointedly as he said that last part. "Anyway, I vowed then and there that I would take you to this place as soon as I could. So, what do you think?"

"It's the most beautiful place I've ever been." I turned around a couple more times, tilting my head back and lifting my arms. "I feel like we are the only two people around. It's wonderful."

He watched me spin around. "I knew you'd love it here." His voice suddenly got a little softer. "So I was thinking… maybe this could be our special place. It's kind of in the middle between my house and your house. You and I could come here together when we want a little time to ourselves, and we could come here individually when either one of us needs some time to think." He looked at me expectantly.

I smiled shyly at him. "I can't think of a better place to be. It's so…peaceful here." My brow furrowed a little as I thought of something. "There could be one problem, though. Do you know who owns this property? I mean, we can't just keep meeting on someone else's property, can we? Wouldn't we have to get permission?"

Will chuckled a little. "Always thinking, aren't you? Actually, I happen to know that this property belongs to one of my dad's childhood friends. My dad was the one who told me I could cut through his property to get to your house. Otherwise, I would have never even gone this way. I wonder if my dad knows about this little clearing. I'll have to ask him about it when I get home." He then placed his hands on the small of my back and pulled me closer to him. "Now that I took care of that question, what do you think?"

I smiled teasingly. "About the clearing or about you?"

He smiled back. "Either one. Both. Take your pick."

I pretended to seriously contemplate his question. "Well, one of the two I think is amazing. The other one I think is the best thing that has ever happened to me." I smiled coyly at him.

He tilted his head and raised one eyebrow. "I'm hoping that I am the second one. Although, I would have to argue that I am also the first one."

I laughed. "Well, you are pretty amazing."

He took one hand and tipped my chin up so that he could look straight into my eyes. That penetrating gaze always made me a little weak in the knees. "Katherine Kensington, you are the most amazing girl I have ever met. I wanted to bring you here so that I could tell you…I think I'm falling in love with you."

Even though I had been feeling the same thing, hearing him say it aloud took the words away from my lips. Being this close to him was making me feel a little dizzy. I just stared at him, unable to form the words that I wanted so desperately to say.

His voice was low and husky as he said, "Don't feel like you have to say anything. I just wanted you to know…" As he said that, he closed his eyes and his lips met mine for the first time.

* * * * * * * * *

"At least the last part of the evening ended up going well!" Nicey said as she laid her knitting project back in her lap.

"I'll say it went well! How incredibly romantic!" Hope swooned, closing her eyes and placing her hand over her heart. "I can't help but wish it were me instead of you," she added wistfully.

"Well, it wasn't you, and it probably never will be you. Don't get your hopes up," Patience said gruffly.

Nicey was looking at her sister strangely. A small smile spread across her lips. "If I didn't know better, Patience, I would say that all your grumpiness is hiding the fact that your eyes are a little misty right now. I think this true love stuff is getting to you after all!"

Patience wiped her eyes a bit with a tissue. "I just had something in my eyes!" she snapped back at her sister. "Can't a person get something in their eyes without getting scrutinized for it?" She seemed as if she had spoken her peace when she added, "And I am not starting to believe in this mushy-mushy-true-love stuff, either!"

Needless to say, no one believed her and they all stifled a giggle. Hope then glanced down at her watch and said, "My goodness! It's after 10:00! That's way past my bedtime!"

Nicey smiled warmly at Katherine. "You tell such a good story, Katherine, that we forget about the time!" She started putting her knitting projects away for the evening and the other sisters followed suit.

Katherine smiled apologetically. "Sorry, ladies. I tried to make it as short as possible, but I had to work the kiss in before the evening was through or I thought one of you might skin me!" She looked pointedly at Patience.

"It was about time you got to that part," Patience mumbled as she started standing up.

Katherine and the other two sisters exchanged an amused glance. As Katherine stood up, she waved and said, "Goodnight, ladies. Sweet dreams. See you in the morning."

After the sisters said "goodnight" to each other and to Katherine, they all walked drowsily to their rooms. As Katherine neared her door, she felt a little tap on her shoulder. She turned around and was surprised to see Patience standing there. "Oh, it's you, Patience...did you need something?"

Patience looked down a little sheepishly. "Well, I was wondering how long it all lasted."

Katherine thought she meant her marriage. "Will and I were married for-"

Patience interrupted her before she could finish. "No, not your marriage. The kiss! How long did your first kiss last?" She looked at Katherine impatiently.

Katherine laughed a little. "Oh, *that*. Well, let's just say that we were almost late for my 8:00 curfew. It was wonderful."

Patience seemed satisfied. "That's what I thought." Then she became her usual critical self. "Why couldn't you have just said that before?" With that, she turned around in a huff and headed off to her room.

Katherine put her hand over her mouth to hide her smile. That Patience was one of a kind. That was certain.

Katherine opened the door to her room and lay down on her bed. It undoubtedly had been a very long evening. She knew that the three sisters were thoroughly enjoying her story, but would soon hear the most tragic part of it. That was the part she dreading. That was the part she wished had never happened at all.

Chapter Ten

KATHERINE WOKE UP the next morning a little later than usual. Her late-night storytelling was certainly taking its toll. She usually got up with the sunrise, but today it was half past six before she got out of bed. She thought she could at least get a quick walk in before breakfast at 8:00, so she hastily put on her walking clothes, laced up her shoes, and headed out her door into the commons area.

She was surprised to see that the commons area was relatively quiet when she walked through. Perhaps the sisters were still catching up on their sleep after last night. She saw John in his usual spot, reading the paper in one of the easy chairs by the sunny bay window on the eastern edge of the room. As she exchanged a good morning nod with John, she saw some movement out of her peripheral vision from the west side of the commons area. She turned her head in time to see Hope emerging from her room. There was no chance of slipping out the door before Hope saw her, so Katherine decided that she may as well greet Hope before she got out on her morning walk.

"Good morning, Hope. You are looking rather chipper this morning. This is earlier than you usually get out of bed, isn't it?" Katherine said with a little gleam in her eye. She glanced over at John reading his newspaper and then back at Hope again.

Hope followed Katherine's line of vision and turned a crimson color. "Oh, umm, good morning, Katherine. Yes, it is a little earlier than I usually get up. I slept so well last night after your romantic story." She moved in a little closer to Katherine and lowered her voice. "I think your story inspired me. I decided I need to take charge of my love life, even if I am past my prime. I heard you say once that you see John reading the paper every morning when you get up for your walk, so I decided I would be in the commons area at the same time and see what happens." She smiled an optimistic smile and then lowered her gaze a little. "There's just one problem. I've never been very good at starting a conversation with a man. I wish I weren't so very shy." She looked over at John and blushed all over again.

Katherine couldn't help but smile. She decided that Hope might need a little help to prod her along in her romantic endeavors. "Hope, how about I introduce you two? I've talked to him multiple times in the morning before going on my walk, so I would feel comfortable enough to do that."

Hope's eyes lit up as she gave Katherine a grateful smile. "You would do that for me? I think that's all I would need is a little help with the introduction part. I think I am good at conversation once I get started." Her voice then got a little hesitant. "Are you sure that it won't seem awkward? I just don't want him to get the wrong first impression about me."

Katherine smiled encouragingly. "I'm sure you've already made some sort of an impression on him just by spending time in the same place together. I happen to have noticed that he looks over here every so often when we are all in the commons.

I think that he may think a certain someone is attractive." Katherine raised her eyebrows suspiciously.

Hope looked down at the ground. "Well, I'm not so sure about that. Maybe he was looking over at you or Nicey. Or Patience."

Both ladies giggled. Hope said, "Okay, maybe not Patience. But maybe one of you two. Anyways, I guess I'll never know unless I try, right?"

"Right. And that's why I need to introduce you two." Katherine took Hope by the hand and led her over to the other side of the commons area to where John was sitting.

John looked up from the variety section and noticed the two ladies standing in front of him. He cleared his throat and stood up. "Well, hello there, ladies. Would you two like to join me?"

Katherine smiled warmly at him. "Good morning, John. Actually, I was just headed out for my morning walk, but I thought you might enjoy some company. I'm not sure if you've met Hope yet. John, Hope. Hope, John."

John smiled and clasped Hope's hand in his. "I don't think we have officially met, although I have noticed you ladies involved in your little knitting projects from across the room. I was hoping I'd get the chance to meet you soon." With that, he gestured for Hope to sit down in the chair facing him.

"Why, thank you. It's nice to meet you, too. Officially, that is." They both smiled as she sat down in the chair adjacent to his.

Katherine interrupted their little interlude. "Well, I better get outside so I can get some sort of a walk in before breakfast! You two have fun," Katherine called out as she walked towards the exit and out the door.

Once outside, Katherine decided to take a route directly northward toward the grove instead of her usual route. She figured she only had about a half an hour before she had to be back in to get ready for the day before breakfast started. Walking at a brisk pace, she approached the grove in less than ten minutes. She noticed that she was approaching from the same direction that she had the first time Will had taken her there.

As she passed through the trees into the clearing, Katherine stopped and closed her eyes. Sometimes she could almost feel Will's presence when she did that. She opened her eyes and looked upward towards the overarching branches above her. The beauty of this place never ceased to amaze her.

She made her way over to her bench by the gravestone. As she sat down, she let her fingers run over the inscription on the front of the bench. "Will loves Katherine," Katherine said aloud as her fingers ran across the all-familiar inscription. She let out a weary sigh. "I never tire of hearing that." She smiled a rueful smile. "I wish I could actually *hear* you say it. Someday..." She looked upward, wanting to somehow diminish the space between her and Will.

Her eyes eventually wandered back to the gravestone. "Well, I told the three sisters part of the story. I've gotten to the part where you took me to this grove and we had our first kiss. I think they liked that part. I know I did." Katherine smiled. "I'm just glad I wasn't late for curfew or my parents would never have given you another chance." Her face clouded over a little. "Although, it's not like my dad ever gave you much of a chance to begin with. I always felt rather badly about that...how he treated you, I mean. But, somehow, you never seemed to let it bother you much. Always the eternal optimist..."

She cleared her throat as she continued. "Soon I'll be getting to the hard part of the story. I wish I could just skip that part, but then they wouldn't understand what really happened and would never see how much you really loved me. Then Patience would never believe in true love, and that, I'm afraid, would be tragic. She needs a little jolt of love in her life. Trust me, if you met her, you would understand." Her eyes looked up thoughtfully. "Maybe you can see her from where you are. If you can, I'm sure you have had plenty of laughs." Katherine chuckled a little at the thought of it. "Anyway, I'm not quite sure I'll know exactly what to say when I get to the part where… well, you know what happened. It's just so…difficult." She let out a long sigh. "But, it needs to be told, and so told it shall be." Katherine closed her eyes and whispered a little prayer. "God, give me the strength to make it through today."

After kissing her fingers and resting them on the gravestone, Katherine made her way down the little path and across the field towards New Horizons. Breakfast would be served soon, and Katherine wanted to hear all about how Hope and John got along that morning. If Katherine's hunches were correct, which they usually were, the two had hit it off and would soon be spending more time together. Nothing would make her happier at this point than if Hope would get her chance at love. After all, true to her name, she had been hoping for love her whole life. It was about time.

Chapter Eleven

As Katherine opened the front doors of New Horizons, she saw Hope and John still engrossed in conversation. Hope glanced up and saw Katherine from across the way, and Katherine gave her an encouraging smile before going into her room to get ready for the day.

Katherine had to hustle a little if she hoped to get to breakfast by 8:00. She had spent a little too long in the grove. It was hard not to. It was the only place she felt truly close to Will. She put on a comfortable pair of slacks and a sweater that Will had always said was one of his favorites. It was an emerald green and illuminated Katherine's green eyes, which were Will's favorite feature of hers. He had admitted early on that her eyes were what had first attracted his attention to her at the dance.

After running a brush through her hair and putting on a little make-up, Katherine made her way out the door and over to the commons area where the three sisters seemed to be engaged in their own little conversation. The breakfast trays were already out and Katherine's was set up by her chair. It looked like French toast, cottage cheese, and some fruit this morning. As she sat down, Nicey and Hope turned towards her with smiles on their faces.

Nicey was the first to speak. "Good morning, Katherine! We have some good news for you." She looked over at Hope as if prodding her to speak.

Hope had a big smile on her face as she leaned in a little and lowered her voice. "John and I talked for over an hour! I couldn't believe it! I've never spoken to a man for that long before. And it was so natural and easy. We talked about everything, from the weather to his wife who passed away to our interests. He really is wonderful to talk to." Her words came rushing out in an excited babble.

Patience didn't seem to share the excitement of her sisters. She seemed a little annoyed. "Well, I don't mean to rain on your parade, but someone has to be the realistic one here. I know I told you this earlier, but I wouldn't get your hopes up. I've seen that man flirting with a few ladies here. Why, you yourself saw him talking with Meg the other day. In my opinion, I think he likes female attention a little too much." She seemed to be getting more and more agitated as she spoke. "I know what can happen when people get emotionally attached and then end up with a broken heart. And don't you think for one minute that I'm going to sit around and watch it all happen!" She then got up and walked to her room, slamming the door as she went in.

The three ladies' eyes were wide in bewilderment of what had just transpired. Katherine stared at the door Patience had just slammed, lost in thought about something that Patience had said. She turned to Nicey. "Nicey, what did she mean by 'she knows what can happen when people get attached and end up with a broken heart'? Was she talking about people in general, or was she talking about herself?"

Nicey and Hope both exchanged a glance. Hope nodded,

as if giving Nicey the okay to go ahead. Nicey sighed. "Well, we weren't going to say anything about it because Patience gets so upset whenever someone brings it up, but she's in her room right now and I think it is something you should know about her before you continue on with your own story. Do you remember that first day that we met you, when we were all in the commons area?"

Katherine nodded. "Yes, I remember that pretty clearly. You were all 'discussing' whether there was such a thing as true love."

Nicey smiled. "That's right. We were 'discussing', as you say, the concept of true love. There's always a discussion when Patience is around, that's for sure. Anyway, if you will recall, I said that I had been married to Henry and completely believed in true love, Hope said that she believed in love but had never found it for herself, and Patience said that she didn't believe and would never believe in true love."

Katherine added, "Actually, I think her exact words were, 'Men are pigs and they are only after a good time and someone to clean up after them.'"

Hope giggled. "You forgot that they are deceptive and smelly."

Nicey chuckled a little. "Yes, her words seem to have made quite the impression." She cleared her throat and her voice got a little more serious. "Anyway, you already know that Patience has never been married and never plans to marry, but what you don't know is that she almost got married once."

A gasp escaped from Katherine. "Really? I would never have guessed. She seems like the type of person who has always wanted to remain single."

Nicey nodded. "She does come off that way. But, you can never truly understand a person until you've heard their whole story. Patience is the way she is now because of what happened when she was young. She used to be…different."

Katherine seemed confused. "How so? It's hard for me to picture her any different than she is now because I've only just met her."

"Well, she wasn't any more patient before, I can assure you of that. She's been a little ball of *im*patience from the day she was born. But, she did used to be open to the concept of love and marriage. I would even venture to say that she enjoyed life and had an overall optimistic view of things." She stopped for a second to let this bit of information sink in.

"Optimistic? I just can't picture Patience fitting that description," Katherine mused.

"I know it's hard to believe, but trust me, it's true," Hope confirmed.

Nicey continued on with her story. "There was one man in particular who really captured her attention. His name was Virgil, and he was a year older than she was. She met him at the end of her junior year in high school, and she soon fell in love. She became convinced that he was the one for her." Nicey paused a bit after this.

"And then what happened?" Katherine prodded.

"Well, Virgil was the type of guy who liked the attention of the ladies. He was athletic, handsome, and outgoing, and he always had girls hanging around who wanted to spend time with him. However, soon after the two started dating, Virgil stopped paying attention to the other ladies and focused on Patience. Because of this, Patience was convinced that he was fully devoted to her, but…" Nicey took a deep breath.

"But what? Did he stay faithful to her?" Katherine asked.

"It's a little difficult to talk about, but like I said earlier, Patience was never really the patient type of person. After about a year of dating, after she graduated from high school, the two began talking about getting married. She was convinced that he would propose any day, but it wasn't soon enough for her. She decided that she couldn't wait to get married, so she...how do I say this? She gave herself to him."

Katherine looked surprised. "You mean she...?" The two sisters nodded. "Oh," Katherine said.

"It may be more common in today's day and age, but back then it was definitely not the norm. My whole family, especially our mother, was very religious, and if she had ever found out about it, she would have chained Patience in the basement and fed her on bread and water."

"So she never found out?" Katherine inquired.

"No, she didn't, but I did. Patience eventually did tell me," Nicey said. "But that was after she discovered...or, she suspected...she was pregnant."

"What?" Katherine gasped. "How did she figure that out?"

"Well, she wasn't feeling very well in the mornings, and then she missed her monthly cycle. She didn't know what to do or whom she could trust, so she came and found me. She was crying and ended up telling me everything."

"Did she eventually tell Virgil?"

"I advised her that she should. It wasn't fair that she had to do it alone. But then, right before she got up the courage to tell him, she found out from a trustworthy friend that Virgil wasn't being as faithful to her as she thought he was. I'm not sure exactly what happened, but all I know is it involved another girlfriend."

"Poor Patience," Katherine said sympathetically. "What did she do then? Whatever happened with the baby?"

"Well, let's just say that one of Patience's other qualities is that she is also very stubborn. She decided that any man who cheated on her didn't deserve her and certainly wouldn't make a good father. She broke up with him and never even told him about the baby. She also made the decision that she would keep the baby. She wasn't sure how that would all work out, but she would never consider abortion, and she didn't want to give it up for adoption."

Katherine's face clouded over in confusion. "Didn't he eventually suspect something? I mean, it's not like it's an easy thing to hide a baby."

"It kind of took care of itself. Patience was still so early along that no one even suspected anything yet. Then, one morning, Patience came to my room with a strange look on her face. I asked her what was going on, and she said that something went wrong while she was in the bathroom. She said that she had started bleeding heavily and thought something was wrong with the baby. I followed her, and sure enough, there was blood all over the bathroom floor. She must have had a miscarriage and her body was getting rid of the aftermath. Obviously, we couldn't just take her to the doctor because nobody knew about the baby, so I helped her clean up the bathroom and then stayed with her the rest of the day while her body finished ejecting all evidence of the baby. We had a little burial for the unborn child in the woods behind our house. No one ever found out what happened. We kept it a secret between the two of us."

"Yeah, and I didn't even find out about it until many years later when Nicey finally told me. We both agreed it must have been an act of God. There's no way that Patience could have raised that baby on her own. Besides that, it would have been a huge family scandal. Nicey made me swear to secrecy, though, so I haven't told a soul," Hope added.

"What happened after that? How did Patience react?" Katherine asked.

Nicey exhaled a weary sigh. "That's when Patience went through her little transformation. She became more withdrawn, even from the two of us. She told me that she vowed to never again trust a man. She said that she would never marry, and true to her word, she hasn't. Where she used to be more of an optimist, she now became the extreme opposite. She saw the negative in every person and in every situation. She became somewhat of a bitter person, which you now see before you today." Nicey took a tissue out of her pocket and dried the tears that were forming in her eyes.

"Which is why she dislikes John already," Katherine noted.

"Yes. In some ways, John seems to be a little like Virgil. He's handsome, outgoing, and smooth around the ladies." Nicey looked at Hope.

"I know, but he really doesn't seem like the type to cheat on people. I mean, he was married to his wife for forty years before she died. That doesn't sound like the cheating kind to me," Hope pointed out.

Nicey patted her hand. "I believe you, dear. It's just that Patience looks at him and sees Virgil, and that, my dear, will make it impossible for her to accept him. You'll just have to know that going into it all."

"I know, and I'll be careful," Hope promised.

Nicey turned her attention back to Katherine. "I'm sure it's been obvious that Patience has some problems trusting and getting along with people. But, underneath it all, she really is a caring and sensitive person. I see it come out every once in a while, even though it usually is hidden far underneath that hardened exterior of hers. As soon as it comes out, though, she is soon to stuff it back underneath with a harsh comment. I think it's her defense mechanism for coping with life."

Katherine seemed to be lost in thought. "I think I saw it come out the other night. Do you remember when we all said goodnight to each other and then went to our rooms last night?" Katherine looked to Nicey and Hope as they nodded. "Well, just before I opened my door to go into my room, I felt a little tap on my shoulder. I turned around, and Patience was standing there. It was a little odd for a couple of reasons. First of all, she never seeks me out to ask me anything. Also, she didn't have her usual scowl on her face. She had an almost childlike inquisitive look on her face, and I could tell she wanted to ask me something."

"What did she ask you?" Hope prodded.

"She asked me how long my first kiss lasted. Actually, she asked how long 'it' lasted, and at first I thought she was referring to the length of my marriage. After we cleared up the misunderstanding of what she was asking about, I told her a little more about our first kiss. She had a little satisfied smile on her face for just a moment, and then she must have realized that I was looking at her a little strangely and she reverted back to her normal pleasant self. I believe she said, 'Why didn't you just say that earlier?'"

The two sisters looked at each other before Nicey commented. "Like I said, you can see it come out every once in a while. I really think she wants to believe that true love can exist, but she was so hurt by Virgil that she won't let herself believe." She paused a little before she looked up wistfully and said, "Maybe it will take your story to make her believe again."

"Oh, yes! That would be a miracle in itself!" Hope added.

Katherine smiled. "I wouldn't put all your eggs in one basket on that one. I hope I can change her mind about love, but I can't guarantee anything. Besides, I haven't gotten to the other parts of the story yet. She may not exactly enjoy all the parts coming up."

Hope's eyes widened as a slight gasp escaped from her mouth. "What do you mean? What could possibly go wrong after that wonderful kiss and you two falling in love?"

Katherine sighed. "Trust me....every love story has its own

set of problems to sort out. Otherwise, it hasn't stood the test of time. My personal theory is that if things are too easy a person doesn't appreciate them as much."

Nicey nodded in agreement. "I completely agree with you on that one. Why, even my own grandkids, as good and sweet as they are, don't appreciate some of the modern conveniences they have that we never used to have around. I tell them how blessed they are all the time, and they don't quite seem to comprehend how lucky they are."

Hope was looking over at John across the room. She seemed to be lost in thought when Nicey coughed to get her attention. She spun her head back around and focused back in on the conversation. "Oh, sorry, dears. I was just thinking. Katherine, I would have to agree with you on your theory as well. I haven't ever found love in my life, and I know beyond a shadow of a doubt that I would appreciate that person ten times more than I would have when I was younger. That is, if I ever find love at this point in my life." She had turned her attention back to John as she said the last statement.

Nicey patted Hope on the leg encouragingly. "Well, things are definitely looking hopeful, aren't they? I mean, you did have the longest talk you've ever had with a man just this morning. That has to mean something."

"And John did say when I introduced you two this morning that he had been hoping to get the chance to meet you soon," Katherine added with a twinkle in her eye.

Hope was smiling by this time. "Yes, I suppose things are looking promising for me, aren't they? Mother didn't name me Hope for nothing!"

The three ladies laughed. Hope then went on to relay exactly what was said that morning in her conversation with John. A half an hour later, they were still assessing Hope's prospects when the large grandfather clock in the commons area chimed eleven o'clock.

Nicey looked over at the clock. "Goodness gracious, how time flies! I wanted to take a little nap and talk to Patience before lunch. I better hurry if I hope to do all that!"

Hope looked a little alarmed. "What exactly are you going to say to her, Nicey? She probably feels embarrassed about running out of the room. And you know how she acts when she's embarrassed about something."

"Yes, she's even more pleasant than usual," Nicey said sarcastically. "That is exactly why I need to go talk to her. I want her to know that we aren't upset at her and that she doesn't need to feel badly about anything."

"I definitely wouldn't mention that we told Katherine about Virgil," Hope added.

"Oh, I most certainly will not mention that. I think that piece of information is better left unsaid. She would never come out of her room if she knew we told Katherine that story."

Katherine looked at the two ladies a little sheepishly. "I promise that I will not mention anything about me knowing about Virgil. We don't need you two getting into trouble with your sister. I want you to know that I am grateful you entrusted me with that story. I feel like I understand Patience a lot better now."

Nicey sighed. "Yes, that is a difficult task to undertake… knowing Patience, that is. She has such a hard time opening up and trusting people, but now you at least understand why. We completely trust you with her story, my dear, or we wouldn't have told you." She smiled at Katherine. "You needed to know."

"I'm glad we told you," Hope chimed in.

Nicey looked over at the clock again and hurriedly got out of her chair. "Sorry to leave so quickly, but I have to get moving if I want to get to lunch on time!" She started heading toward

Patience's room. Before she got to the door, she looked back over her shoulder and whispered, "Wish me luck!"

"Good luck!" Katherine and Hope said in unison.

After Nicey went into Patience's room, Hope turned her attention back to Katherine. "Just to let you know, it probably would be best to pretend like nothing happened when Patience comes out later. She doesn't handle embarrassment very well, I'm afraid. She gets extra spiteful because she is trying to cover her true feelings up."

"Good to know. I will pretend like nothing happened. Maybe I'll just pick up my story from where I left off last night," Katherine offered.

"That would be perfect. I am all but dying to know what happens in your story now that you told us that there were a few bumps in the road."

"Guess you'll just have to wait until after lunch," Katherine said mysteriously.

"I suppose you can't just tell me the story without the other two here. Well, I wouldn't stop you or anything, but Nicey and Patience might not like it too much. And we definitely don't need to give Patience anything else to be upset about!"

Katherine laughed. "No, we don't." She looked at the clock as she stifled a yawn. "I think that nap that Nicey mentioned earlier is sounding good right about now. I think that late night we had last night has taken its toll on my body! I usually don't feel very tired during the day, but I sure do feel sleepy now. I'll see you at lunch, Hope."

"That's fine. I think I have a few things I need to take care of." Hope looked towards John and gave Katherine a little smile.

"Oh, I see. Important things." Katherine winked at Hope. "Let me know how it goes."

"How what goes?" Hope said innocently as she started

making her way over to the other side of the room where John was.

Katherine had a smile on her face as she walked towards her door. These three sisters sure kept things interesting.

CHAPTER TWELVE

LUNCH WAS AT 12:30 that day, and shortly before that time people were filing into the commons to find their seats. Katherine was out her door before any of the three sisters made an appearance. She made her way to her chair, picked up the local newspaper, and began to skim it over for the recent news. She hadn't gotten past the front page when she saw Hope and John emerge through the front door. Hope had a huge smile on her face as she thanked John for the walk and made her way over to Katherine.

Hope sat down in her chair, waited for John to get out of hearing distance, and let out an excited squeal to Katherine. "You'll never guess what happened!" She paused for dramatic effect. "When you went into your room to take your nap before lunch, I just happened to saunter over by John. He said hello and we made polite conversation, and then he asked me if I wanted to go for a little walk outside. You know what that means, don't you?"

Katherine looked a little perplexed. She wasn't sure what

Hope was getting at. "Well, it could mean a number of things. You tell me."

"He wanted to get me alone, you see! Besides that, walks are so romantic! I mean, in your story that's when Will took you to that little grove and kissed you for the first time. Then…"

Katherine interrupted her, raising one eyebrow suspiciously. "Is that what happened on your walk?"

Hope flushed a deep shade of red. "Oh, no. We don't know each other *that* well yet. I mean, I *wish* that is what happened. But something else exciting did happen!" She squealed again and clapped her hands like an excited child.

Katherine couldn't help but smile at Hope's enthusiasm. "Well, go on! What was it?"

Hope's eyes got wide with excitement. "He asked me out on a *date*. A real genuine date. Can you imagine? I haven't been on a date in…well, too many years to count right now." Suddenly her forehead creased in a worried expression. "Oh, Katherine, I won't know what to do or say or wear." She paused and looked down at her body as if mentally assessing her wardrobe and the possibilities for her date. She looked at Katherine and clutched her throat despairingly. "What if I make a fool of myself and he decides that he's not interested anymore? Oh, my goodness! Maybe this isn't such a good idea after all!"

Katherine patted her leg encouragingly. "Now, don't get all worried about it. You have three people here to help you." She paused as she saw Patience come out of her room and changed her statement. "Well, maybe two people to help you. But that's more than enough! We will help you with getting ready and anything else you need." Katherine made her voice a little softer. "Trust me, he wouldn't have asked you out if he wasn't interested."

Hope seemed to evaluate this before answering. "I guess you're right. I'm just a little nervous." She saw Patience getting closer and whispered, "We better talk about this later. Patience won't approve, and I don't want to upset her again."

Katherine nodded as Patience sat down. She remembered what Hope had said earlier about pretending like Patience's outburst hadn't happened. Deciding the best course was maybe not to say anything at all, she busied herself in perusing the paper once again.

Patience looked over at Hope and Katherine and decided she was going to be the first one to speak. "Have either of you two seen Nicey?" She looked over at the clock. "It's nearly 12:30. She's going to miss lunch!" She let out an irritated huff and looked over at Nicey's door just as she opened it and came out.

Nicey walked a little stiffly over to her chair and sat down. "Sorry I'm a little late, ladies. I didn't have very long before lunch, but I wanted to try to get a nap in anyway. Once I finally fell asleep, I must have slept pretty hard because I barely heard my alarm go off!"

"Well, it's about time! We were just about to go in after you!" Patience snapped.

Nicey smiled at her short-tempered sister good-naturedly and said, "How touching! You were so worried about me that you wanted to check on me! It's nice to know you care so much." She looked over at her sister, receiving a disdainful look as she continued. "Hmmm…it's either that, or Patience here can't wait for the next installment of Katherine's story! Maybe it's a little of both!"

Patience snorted. "You can think what you want to think. I wasn't worried. I was just curious as to where you were." She paused a little before continuing on. "Katherine here was going to start in on her story again, so she would probably want you here." Nicey was still smiling as she kept teasing Patience. "Ah, so you didn't want me to miss the story. How sweet of you!"

"No, I just didn't think that Katherine would start without you, and you know how much Hope wants to hear the rest of the story," Patience stated matter-of-factly.

"Of course, *you* don't want to hear the rest of the story, do you, Patience?" Nicey said with a mischievous twinkle in her eye.

"Well, I wouldn't *mind* hearing some more. That is, if she wants to tell more of it." She made her voice very nonchalant. "She may as well since we're all here and everything."

"You don't fool us for one second, Patience." Nicey paused to thank the staff members as they brought the ladies their lunch trays. "Well, Katherine, you may as well get on with it since two of us are interested in hearing what happens next."

Katherine tried to suppress a smile as she began her story once again.

* * * * * * * * *

After our first kiss in the grove, I knew that I couldn't deny the fact that I was falling in love with Will, too. I still hadn't told him verbally that I felt the same way, but it was as if Will knew what I was feeling without me actually saying it. He had an uncanny ability read into the depths of my being.

Unfortunately, my parents suspected how serious my feelings were for Will as well, and they didn't like the way our relationship was headed. They didn't say a lot in front of me, but I heard them talking about it on a few occasions. One time, about a month after Will and I had kissed in the grove, my parents thought I was upstairs sleeping when I overheard a conversation of theirs. I had gone downstairs to get a drink of water since I couldn't sleep very well, and I paused at the door of the study because I heard some voices. They were speaking in hushed tones, but I could still hear what they were saying.

My father's voice was the first that I heard. "Well, Carolyn, I think we need to do something. It's obvious to both of us that Katherine and this…farmer boy…are getting very serious very quickly. If we keep waiting it out and choose to do nothing, the next thing we'll know Katherine will be telling us that they are getting married!"

Then my mother spoke, trying to calm my father down. "Now, Michael, don't go jumping to any conclusions. They've only been dating for about two months! I think it's just a case of puppy love. Everyone has it in high school. I'm sure they'll break up sometime soon. Then our Katherine can go off to finishing school as we've planned and settle down with someone more suitable for her."

I couldn't believe my ears. I knew deep down that they didn't approve of Will for me, but knowing it and hearing them say it were two very different things.

My father spoke again. "I'm just not sure that it's 'puppy love' as you say. I see the way those two look at each other. It seems more serious than that." He let out an agitated sigh. "Why would Katherine even go for someone like him? He's not anything like the kind of person we…or she…has ever envisioned for herself. She's always enjoyed our lifestyle. I naturally assumed she would meet someone like…well, like us…someone who fits into our family and our position in society."

It was my mother's turn to sigh. "Well, Michael, what do you propose we do about it? Should we forbid her to see him?" She soon answered herself. "No, we couldn't do that. She would just rebel and go the other way. We don't want to lose her completely. She's our only daughter…our only child. And William really is a nice young man…"

My father coughed. "You mean you like him? You can't possibly mean that you think he's good enough for our daughter!"

"I never said he was good enough for our Katherine, but you have to admit that he is a fine young man in his own right."

There was a pause as if my father was considering what she said and weighing his next words. "He is a decent fellow, but he isn't up to my standards for our daughter. Someone has to watch out for her future. We need to do something before it's too late. I thought of forbidding her to see him as well, but like you say, she might turn against us because of it. Perhaps we should… limit…Katherine's time with him. We certainly could limit her time on the telephone. I have some important business calls that come in during the evening, so we could use that as a reason to keep the line open. We could also keep her so busy around here that she won't have time for him."

My mother broke in to add some of her own suggestions. "She could certainly help me with the Summerville Ladies' Society. There are always things to be done there. Why, we have a benefit coming up this next month. She can help me make decorations and preparations for that. School will be starting shortly after the benefit, so we shouldn't have a problem keeping her busy then with all of her lessons and studies." She made a gasp like she just thought of something. "We could also introduce Katherine to other young men. In fact, Thomas and Marie Wellington have a son about Katherine's age…Richard, I believe his name is. We could arrange a meeting with him sometime soon." She was really beginning to get excited now. "Why, I could telephone Marie tomorrow afternoon and figure something out."

The firm voice of my father came through loud and clear. "Yes, I think it's about time Katherine started hanging out with young men a little more her caliber. It's about time William Brenner got out of the picture."

I heard my father's feet hit the floor as if he were getting up. If I didn't move quickly, my father would find me outside the study door and I would have some serious explaining to do. I started tiptoeing up to my bedroom as swiftly and as quietly as I could. I crawled in my bed just as I heard the door to the study open.

I pulled the covers over my head, trying to shut out the pain I was feeling inside. Part of me wished I had never overheard the conversation, but another part of me knew that I needed to have heard it. Why did everything have to be so difficult? Why couldn't my parents accept Will for who he was? Didn't they want me to be happy?

I slowly pushed the covers down from around my face. My parents may have surmised correctly about my feelings for Will, but if they thought I would give him up that easily, they were far underestimating my determination to see our relationship succeed. Will wasn't a part of my life that I could just cut off and then start anew; his life was now intertwined with mine in such a way that any severing would cut off a piece of myself as well.

I resolved then and there that the moment my parents chose to put their plan in action, they were no longer any parents of mine. Yes, I would still do my best to live in their household as peacefully as possible, but I was waging an internal war. A war for my heart. And I would win.

* * * * * * * * *

Hope gasped. "Oh, Katherine, you poor thing. That must be what you meant when you said there were some bumps in the road in your relationship."

Katherine smiled a weary smile. "Actually, these are just the roadbumps compared to the mountains that are soon to come in the story."

Hope put her hand over her chest. "Can it possibly get any worse? I'm not sure if I can stand any more of this. I do hope you get the sad parts over with soon. It does have a happy ending, doesn't it?"

Patience broke in, annoyed as usual. "Well, of course it has a happy ending! Do you think she would tell it to us if it didn't?" She then looked doubtfully at Katherine and lowered her voice a little. "It does have a happy ending, doesn't it?"

All four ladies laughed. Nicey said, "We'll never get to the good parts if we keep interrupting, will we? Keep going, Katherine, and we'll try to keep our mouths shut."

"Well, I know *I* can keep my mouth shut," Patience said pointedly.

Nicey and Hope rolled their eyes as Katherine took this as a good time to continue on before an argument broke out.

* * * * * * * * *

As you can imagine, I had the most difficult time sleeping after knowing what my parents had brewing. Finally, the pink rays of the sun began to peek through my bedroom window. I decided I may as well get up, for there was no hope of sleeping now.

I was dying to tell Will what I had discovered, but I wasn't sure how to go about it. My parents, true to their word, would be limiting my time on the telephone. I was sure my mother would be making her list of things for me to do each day in an effort to keep me from Will.

It was just after six when I came down the steps, dressed and ready for the day to begin. My mother was in the living room, sipping on a cup of tea. She smiled at me as I descended the last few steps.

"How did you sleep, darling?"

I tried to detect any hint of conspiracy or betrayal in her voice. Detecting none, I started to wonder if perhaps what I had heard last night was simply a dream. I was about to answer her question when she started speaking again.

"Dear, come sit down next to me." She patted the spot next to her on the sofa. "I have a few things I wanted to speak to you about."

Piquing my curiosity, I came around the sofa and sat down. "Yes, Mother?"

She cleared her throat before starting. "I have been thinking lately that maybe you would be interested in aiding me in a few things. You have so much free time in the summer, and I thought you might be getting a little bored."

The prior night's conversation between my parents came rushing through my mind before I could stop it. I tried to keep the pain I felt inside from appearing on my face. This must be the way my parents were going to go about it. They would pretend to themselves and to me that they were doing this for my own good. I pretended to think over what she said. "Actually, I haven't been bored. I have really enjoyed spending time with my…friends…and there's really not that much of the summer left." Not wanting her to suspect anything, I quickly added, "But I would be glad to help you with some small tasks if you need it, Mother."

She took that as a big "yes" and began to go on and on about all of the things I could do to help her, beginning with preparations for the Summerville Ladies' Society benefit all the way to helping my cousin Lucille prepare for her wedding that was two months away. When she was done with that whole gamut of things to be done, she moved on to her next topic. "Dear, there is also something else that might be amusing for you this summer. I haven't seen my friend Marie for a while now. You remember her, don't you? She lives in Lexington, a little jaunt from here, and I thought it would be exciting to have her over for an afternoon. She has a son named Richard who is your age, and I thought you could perhaps get to know him while I am having tea with Marie. How does that sound to you?"

My mother made it sound as if it was completely spontaneous on her part to think of introducing me to Richard, but I knew better. I knew there was no way I could tell my mother "no" without rousing her suspicion that I knew something. I worded my reply carefully. "I do remember Marie. I think it would be wonderful for you to have her over to catch up with her. However, it sounds as if I will be so busy doing all of those things on your list to help you that I may not have time to socialize with Richard. Perhaps Marie would rather come by herself."

Mother coughed a bit as she was sipping her tea but quickly regained her composure. "Oh, you would have the whole afternoon at your leisure in which to socialize. I didn't mean I would keep you that busy that you wouldn't have any spare time."

Just so busy that I can't see Will', I thought bitterly. I really couldn't see any way out of this, so I gave a noncommittal answer. "I suppose if I'm home, I could visit with Richard for a little while. It might not be very long, though, with all of the things I have to do."

My mother couldn't hide her excitement. Her smile lit up her entire face. "Oh, I'm sure you'll get along splendidly with Richard. He's your age in school, and I've heard he's quite the catch." Her eyes shone with a conspiratorial gleam, as if she were letting me in on an exciting secret.

I feigned a smile, hoping to placate my mother, and then excused myself. Breakfast wouldn't be served for a while yet, but I needed to escape to find someplace to think. I went outside onto the veranda and sat down on the rocking chair. It had always been a soothing place for me to come when my mind was mulling something over. As the rocking motion did its magic for me, I considered different alternatives for handling this situation. My mother was a force to be reckoned with when she was on a mission, and I knew it would become more and more difficult to find times to talk with Will on the phone or to spend time with him. I had to come up with something.

I thought perhaps I could call Susan and have her give Will messages for me. My parents wouldn't object to me calling one of my friends. I considered the possibilities of that option, but finally decided that might not be my best alternative. Susan didn't see Will very often, and I wasn't sure if I wanted to entrust my messages to someone else, even if Susan was incredibly trustworthy.

Another option came to mind. Yes, this idea had merit. Will was working with his father all day on the farm, as usual, but after supper I could to go for a brief walk and meet Will in the grove. Yes, the grove would be the key, as I would soon explain to Will as I told him about my plan. This plan would work. It had to.

CHAPTER THIRTEEN

"WELL, WHAT WAS the plan?" Patience interrupted. "You didn't say what it was!"

Nicey started laughing. "I thought you just told us that you could keep your mouth shut, Miss 'I'm not going to interrupt like my two sisters'! Well, look at you now!"

Patience shot her sister a glare that could have melted an ice cube. "I *was* being quiet. She isn't telling the story correctly!"

Hope gave a little gasp. "Patience, you little devil. Who are you to say she isn't telling the story right?" She looked at Katherine apologetically. "Sorry, Katherine. I think you are doing a wonderful job of telling the story."

Katherine chuckled good-naturedly. "No offense taken. I was just trying to build some suspense in the story." She looked at a pouting Patience. "I will try not to make it quite so suspenseful coming up. Deal?"

"Deal. Otherwise, you are practically *asking* for people to interrupt, you know," Patience stated smugly.

"Only people who have no patience to begin with!" Nicey scolded.

Hope looked at the clock and back at Katherine. "Well, go on, Katherine. There's only a little over an hour left before dinner. We have to hear about the plan."

* * * * * * * * *

Before supper that evening, I asked my mother if I could use the telephone briefly. We had worked on brainstorming and planning for the benefit all afternoon, so I hadn't had a moment to myself. She shot me a suspicious look before replying. "May I ask whom you are calling?"

So that was how it was going to be. "Does it matter, Mother?" came my somewhat cheeky response. I quickly checked myself and added, "Sorry. You just usually don't ask."

She passed it off with a wave of her hand. "I was just curious, that's all. Can't a mother be interested in her daughter's life?" she asked innocently.

She certainly wasn't fooling me. "I thought I would call Susan, and then talk to Will for a bit."

She seemed to consider this before responding. "Your father will be home in about fifteen minutes, and then we'll be having supper. Make sure you are off the phone before he gets home."

It was a good thing I didn't need to speak to Will for very long. Most of what I had to say would happen in the grove later. Speaking in hushed tones so that my mother couldn't overhear, I asked him if we could meet after dinner. He seemed to sense the urgency in my voice, but wisely didn't ask any questions.

I then called Susan, mostly because I had told my mother I would be calling her, and I didn't want to lie to her if I could help it. Though I desperately wanted to tell her about what I had discovered, I stuck to safe topics such as what I had been up to the past few days and school starting soon, fearing my mother would overhear and know that I somehow knew of their plan.

I tried to keep my voice light and carefree so Susan wouldn't suspect anything. I said goodbye to her as my father pulled in the gates.

I heard my father ask my mother how the day had gone, and I knew he was talking about how it had gone with me. She replied that it had gone well, and then went into how I had agreed to meet Richard sometime soon. He seemed pleased with that.

After supper was done, I asked my parents if I could go for a little stroll outside. My father's eyebrows shot up suspiciously. "How long will you be gone?"

"Oh, about an hour," I replied. I could see my father doing the math in his head. He knew that Will's house was a little less than three miles away, and he knew I couldn't get there and back within an hour. That's why the grove was so perfect. He smiled, "I've always been a big believer in the fact that a walk helps clear the mind. Be back before the hour so we don't have to worry about you."

"I sure wouldn't want to worry you," I said sweetly as I grabbed my shawl and headed out the door. The only thing they were worried about was keeping me from Will.

Walking the same route that Will had taken me the first time he had taken me to the grove, I kept a brisk pace in order to reserve as much time as possible for us to talk. Our time together, no matter how brief, was precious now considering the circumstances. I found the little path we had forged through the field and then saw the grove of trees open up before my eyes. Like the first time, it took my breath away. The trees arched over the little clearing in the middle, and for the time being it felt like this grove was a world apart from the one in which I lived, the one with controlling parents and complications and deception.

Will hadn't arrived yet, so I found a stump in the middle of the clearing and sat down to wait for him. The grove began to perform its magic on me, calming my spirit and quieting my mind. I slowly closed my eyes and breathed in deeply. For a brief moment, I felt completely at peace, but then a phrase spoken by my father the prior night snaked its way into the forefront of my thoughts. Though I tried to forget it, my father's voice echoed in my head: *It's about time William Brenner got out of the picture.*

Will ambled into the grove from the opposite direction from which I had come. He took my hands in his as I stood up to greet him. I feigned a smile, but he saw right through it. There was no use trying to hide anything from him. His eyes looked searchingly into mine. "Kate, what is it? Your voice sounded upset on the phone."

Though I had promised to myself that I wouldn't, I erupted into tears at the sound of his voice. He folded me in his arms as I softly sobbed into his chest, exorcising the pain that I had been holding within me. He held me like that for several minutes until I picked my head up and looked into his eyes. All I could say was, "Oh, Will..."

Will sat me down on the stump near us and he sat down on the ground by my feet. He reached up and grabbed my hand, rubbing it gently as I summoned the courage to tell him what I had learned.

As I told him about my parents' conversation the prior evening, his eyes never strayed from mine, even during the difficult parts where I explained that my parents thought he wasn't ever going to be good enough for me. I finished by telling him about their plan to keep me so busy that I would barely ever have time to see him. I let out a big sigh as I finished, mentally exhausted by the mere telling of our awful predicament.

Will brushed the last few tears off of my face, smiling up at me sympathetically. He still maintained his calm demeanor, refusing to allow even something like this to shake him. "Kate, did you really think your parents would ever think of me as an acceptable match for you? Remember, you were the one who was afraid to invite me over for dinner for the first time because of how your father would treat me. It really isn't any surprise that they feel this way."

I looked down at the ground. "I know, but it was a bit of a shock to hear them actually *say* it. And it was a surprise that they were actually concocting a plan behind our backs to keep the two of us apart." My voice had a frustrated edge to it. "The whole thing is just so...devious and deceptive."

Will chuckled softly at my apparent frustration. "Okay, I have to admit that their plan is a little surprising. Even though I knew your dad didn't like me already. I mean, it's not like he hid it or anything when I came over for dinner."

Now he got me to laugh. "I guess that's true. He could have at least *tried* to hide his feelings about you."

"So what do you think we should do about it? You said something about a plan on the phone."

I looked up into the overarching branches thoughtfully. "Well, I thought that since this grove is our special place and it's almost a halfway point between our two houses, this could be our secret meeting spot. Each time we are able to get together, we can meet here to avoid any suspicion. Before departing, we can plan our next meeting time. I know your father will let you meet me anytime you aren't helping him on the farm, and I know my parents will let me out of the house to go on walks multiple times during the week. If one of us isn't able to meet at the prearranged time, we can leave a message for each other on this."

I pulled a small bundle out from under my skirt that I had smuggled from home and opened it up. Inside, I had a small notebook and a pencil within a small metal tin. "Then, whenever the other person is able to get here, there will be a little message for them and a time for the next meeting." I looked down at Will. "So, what do you think?"

Will's eyes lit up as he smiled at me. It was difficult not to feel better when looking at his contagious smile. "I guess you have it all worked out, don't you?" He laughed to himself. "When did you have time to think all this up, may I ask?"

"Oh, sometime after my mother informed me of all the things she had on my list in order to keep me busy until school begins. Oh, and after she told me about meeting Richard," I said sarcastically.

Will's eyebrows shot up amusedly. "And who is Richard?"

"Oh, just some guy my mother and father want to set me up with. I'm sure he's just their type: rich, full of himself, and from a 'perfect' family. I can't wait." My voice was dripping with disgust.

Will feigned an anxious look. "So what you're saying is I have a lot to be worried about."

I laughed. "Oh yes, I'd be extremely worried if I were you." My voice got a little more serious. "Actually, I think Richard is the one who should be a little bit worried. My parents may be able to force me to spend time with him, but they can't control my thoughts. The whole time I'm with him, I'll be wishing I was with you. I can't imagine I'll be too much fun for him to be around."

Will stood up and reached out his hands to pull me up from the stump. He put his arms behind my back and held me close to him. It always made me feel a bit dizzy when he did that. "I guess your parents should think twice before trying to pull one over on you."

I lifted my chin defiantly. "Yes, they should. I decided that I wasn't going to give you up without a fight. And I am definitely going to win this one."

Will reached up with one hand and ran his fingers through

my hair. "No, *we* are going to win this one. What we have is too special for either of us to give up without a fight." The raw tenderness of his voice took my breath out from within me.

My voice came out weakly. "So maybe we can meet here tomorrow at the same time?"

"I'll be here. Waiting for my Kate." As he said that, his lips met mine and the worries of my day melted away before me.

* * * * * * * * *

Hope sighed. "Another kiss. I like hearing about those."

Nicey chimed in. "Yes, you can tell about those any time." She put her head back on the chair and closed her eyes. "It reminds me of Henry and myself when we were young and in love."

Patience looked like she was about to gag. "Yuck! Who wants to hear about that?"

Nicey looked a bit offended. "What do you have against Henry? I thought you liked him!"

"Well, I liked him, but I certainly don't want to hear about you two swapping spit! It's kind of gross when it's your sister," Patience shot back.

The dinner bell interrupted their argument once again. Nicey looked at her middle sister irritably. "It's a good thing the dinner bell rang, or you would have gotten an earful! I need to go wash up before dinner. I'll just pretend you didn't say anything against my Henry."

Patience mumbled something under her breath as she got up out of her chair. "I think I'll go to my room for a bit before dinner, too."

Nicey and Patience went to their rooms, leaving Katherine and Hope sitting in the commons. Hope's eyes wandered over to the other side of the room, and, seeing John, turned a light shade of red.

Katherine followed her line of sight and smiled at Hope. "Well, go on. You two have a date to discuss. I want more details later!"

Hope gave Katherine a thankful smile. "Oh, I definitely will. I didn't want to leave you by yourself, but since you insist, I'll go talk to him. See you at dinner!"

Katherine decided she would go freshen up a bit while Hope talked to John. She would need as much freshening up as possible for the next part of her story.

CHAPTER FOURTEEN

ABOUT FIFTEEN MINUTES later, Katherine reappeared in the commons area. Seeing Nicey already seated in the cluster of chairs, Katherine made her way over and sat down to chat for a bit before the other ladies appeared. Katherine scanned the room for Hope and John, and finally saw them seated over by the bay window on the other side of the commons.

She leaned over towards Nicey and lowered her voice to a whisper. "I know Hope hasn't had a chance to tell you yet because Patience has always been around, but she had a little talk with John this morning." Nicey's eyebrows shot up excitedly. "You don't say. What did they talk about? How did it go?"

"Well, I only got the condensed version because Patience came out of her room shortly after Hope started telling me about it, but to make a long story short, he asked her out on a date!" Katherine smiled giddily.

Nicey gasped. "He did? Well, good for her. She has been waiting to go on another date for...well, too many years, that's for sure. I bet she is so excited." Her eyes got a little wider. "And nervous. We will have to help her out, I think."

Katherine laughed. "Yes, she is definitely both excited and nervous. And she's already asked for our help. She's a little nervous that she won't have anything attractive to wear, and she's also worried about making a fool of herself in front of him. I told her that he wouldn't have asked her out in the first place is he wasn't interested, and she seemed to feel a little bit better after that."

Nicey nodded. She looked at Katherine pensively. "We both know that Hope is a beautiful person inside and out, but she has never really been confident in herself. I wish she could see herself the way we all see her. She deserves to be truly happy, even if her ship comes in later than most people's."

Katherine looked over at the other side of the commons once again, and saw that Hope seemed to be saying goodbye to John and making her way over towards them. She turned to Nicey. "Here she comes. I told her to get more details on their upcoming date before dinner, so I bet she'll have some news for us."

As Hope sat down in her chair next to the ladies, she was grinning ear to ear.

Nicey prodded her. "Well?"

Hope looked over at Katherine questioningly. "Did you fill Nicey in on what's been going on?"

Katherine nodded. "I just gave her the scoop. We're waiting for an update!"

Hope giggled excitedly. She leaned in and said, "We decided on Friday!"

Nicey's eyes widened. "You mean this coming Friday? That's only three days away!"

Hope nodded. "Yes! I know it's coming up soon, but John

said he had somewhere he wanted to take me this Friday, so what could I say to that but yes?"

"Where did he say he was going to take you?" Katherine asked.

"Actually, he didn't say exactly. I think he wants it to be kind of a surprise. I do love surprises!"

"We'll have to help you coordinate your outfit and help you get ready before you go out," Nicey suggested.

Hope gave her sister a grateful look. "Oh, that would be wonderful. I am rather nervous about it all. I just haven't been on a date for so long. And I do so want this to work out."

"We do, too," Nicey said encouragingly.

Just then, Patience poked her head out of her door and sauntered out into the commons area.

Hope leaned towards the other two ladies and whispered, "We'll have to talk more about this later. You-know-who is coming."

The three ladies leaned back in their chairs and tried to look nonchalantly around the room. Patience sat down in her chair and looked at them all suspiciously. "You three are up to something. I just know it. I can sense these things."

The three ladies looked at each other and tried to look innocent. Patience wasn't buying it.

"Oh, you can pretend all you like that you don't know what I'm talking about, but I have my ways of finding out. Just you wait," she warned.

Hope looked torn, but then decided to fill her in. "You have to promise not to be mad first, and then I'll tell you."

"Me? Mad? I won't get mad!" Patience said irritably.

"See? You're already mad. You have to promise," Hope insisted.

"Okay, okay, I promise." Patience held up her hand like she was swearing on the Holy Bible in court or something.

"Well, John asked me out on a date this morning, and I said yes. We are going out this Friday. Nicey and Katherine here are going to help me get ready, and you are invited to help if you want to. But if you do, you have to promise not to be grumpy and ruin my evening before it even starts."

The ladies could tell that Patience was trying to bite her tongue because she had promised not to get mad. She suppressed whatever it was that she had wanted to say and simply said, "Well, I hope you two have a good time together."

Now it was Nicey's turn to be suspicious. "That's really all you have to say? You usually have a lot more to say than that!"

"Well, I did promise to be nice. I do hope they have a good time on their date. I just don't think it's very likely to happen."

Hope seemed taken aback. "What do you mean by that, Patience?"

"I claim the right to keep my opinions to myself for now," Patience said quietly.

The other three ladies decided to leave it at that as the dinner was now being served. Nicey, trying to change the subject, said, "This looks delicious! Baked chicken and mashed potatoes… two of my favorite things!"

The other ladies agreed as they all began to nibble on their dinners. Hope turned towards Katherine and said, "I think we all need to hear a little more about how things turned out for you and Will meeting secretly in the grove. I sure like hearing about those kisses!"

Katherine smiled at Hope as she began her tale once again.

* * * * * * * * *

After I told Will about my plan to meet in our little grove, we managed to meet multiple times a week. We never got to meet for very long, but we met often enough to keep our relationship growing, continually fanning the ember of love that had been lit within both of us. Of course, we both would have wanted to meet more frequently, but that simply wasn't possible without rousing suspicion. As with all who are young and in love, the amount of time you have together never seems to be enough no matter how much you see each other.

During those little secret meetings, I made it my goal to learn as much about Will as possible. For instance, I learned that Will's favorite color was green, his favorite meal was meatloaf and mashed potatoes, the person besides me with whom he preferred to spend time the most in this world was his father, and he was secretly scared of bats. He had only revealed that last one after I had pressured him to tell me something that frightened him, since nothing in this life ever seemed to upset him. I had to laugh because shortly after he had told me that, a bat swooped down near his head at dusk before we were parting, and he nearly knocked me over when he attempted to duck out of the way.

One of the best things about our plan was that my parents didn't suspect anything. That had been one of my only concerns about meeting secretly in the grove. One thing that helped our situation was that I had always been one to go on walks, so my parents didn't think anything of it when I asked to go a few times a week. I was never gone for much more than an hour, so they wouldn't have seriously considered harboring any suspicion that I was visiting Will during my walks. I think my mother assumed I needed a little time out of the house after the rigor of our afternoon activities that she carefully planned each day. My father was a firm believer in exercising the body and the mind, so he never said much either.

A few weeks before school was to start the inevitable happened. Mother invited her friend Marie over for tea, and sure enough, Richard came as well. My mother had bought me a flattering dress for the occasion, and though I didn't want to admit it, I liked the way it looked on me. It had some green accent ribbons that matched the color of my eyes. I would have much rather worn it for Will, but Richard would have to do.

I sat with my mother in the parlor, counting away the minutes until Richard would come and go and I could see my Will again. I think Mother mistook my agitated state for anticipation of Richard's arrival, and nothing could have pleased her more.

Soon enough, the gates opened and our butler announced the arrival of Mrs. Wellington and son. We stood as they were ushered into the parlor, and my mother gave a warm welcome to Marie as Richard appeared from behind his mother. His eyes perused over me, and a small smile appeared on his face, obviously liking what he saw.

My mother then turned towards the two of us to make a formal introduction. I gave a little curtsy as she said my name and Richard returned the favor with a small bow. We all sat down on the parlor chairs as the maids brought in tea and our mothers started in on the local gossip and social events that were coming up.

As they were talking, I had time to look Richard over. He was of average height and build with jet-black hair and eyes almost the same color. His eyes emitted a sense of intelligence as well as something else I couldn't quite put my finger on…it was almost an underlying coldness. His demeanor exuded a sense of absolute confidence in himself. He was what most people would consider extremely attractive, though I had eyes for no one but Will. He was listening politely to our mothers' conversation, and after a few minutes turned his attention towards me.

"Perhaps we should find a place where the two of us could talk," he whispered across the table.

I was slightly appalled by his presumptuousness on a couple

of counts. First of all, teenagers of opposite genders were not usually allowed to be by themselves for any lengthy period of time. Second of all, his assumption that I would want to be with him alone irritated me.

My mother must have overheard his question, and if she thought it was at all inappropriate, her face didn't show it. She turned towards me and said, "Katherine, perhaps you two would like to sit on the veranda and get to know each other a little bit more."

My inner irritation then shifted towards my mother. If Will had been over, she never would have suggested that we sit on the veranda by ourselves to "get to know each other." However, since it was Richard, her obvious choice for me, she was allowing it.

I tried to keep the annoyance out of my voice. I did want to sit on the veranda, but not with Richard. Nevertheless, it was the lesser of two evils. It was better than sitting and listening to my mother talk with Marie. I put a smile on my face. "Yes, Mother."

We both stood and Richard gestured with his arm to let me lead the way to the veranda. *'Oh, so he thinks he's so polite now,'* I thought to myself cynically. *'Well, I better make the best of this, since he's going to be here a while,'* I determined as we headed out the front door.

I headed for the rocking chair, since I thought it might calm me down and help me not to say anything I might regret. Even though I was a little bitter about the whole situation and was angry at my parents, I had a solid enough of a head on my shoulders to realize that Richard was really an innocent party in all of this, even if he did seem somewhat arrogant. He didn't deserve my bitterness. He was as much a pawn in this situation as I was.

Richard took a seat in a chair next to me and smiled at me amusedly. His black eyes seemed to harbor some hidden delight as his smile widened. He cleared his throat. "And so we finally meet, Katherine Kensington. My mother has told me much about you. I was wondering when I was going to have the pleasure of meeting you in person."

I wasn't sure what to make of that. I simply said, "And so we do. My mother has told me quite a bit about you as well." I sipped my tea, having nothing more to offer for the moment.

He took a sip of his tea as well and set it down on the ledge. He turned his piercing black eyes to me once again. "Tell me a little about yourself, Katherine."

I wasn't sure I liked the way my name rolled off of his tongue. It made me sound as if I were something to be studied rather than someone to be known. It irritated me enough that I gave him a somewhat cheeky response. "Since your mother has told you so much about me, why don't you tell me what you think I'm like?"

He smiled mischievously at me, as if accepting the challenge. "Well, for one, you are a rather beautiful creature."

He looked over at me, anticipating some sort of flattered response. He was going to have to use a word other than *creature* if he wanted that. Seeing no reaction other than a raised eyebrow on my part, he continued on.

"You are highly independent and somewhat of a free spirit."

He glanced over at me again. Though he had me pegged correctly, I still gave him no indication that he was reading me correctly.

"You find me somewhat arrogant and are annoyed at me right now." The amused smile returned to his lips as he paused for a reaction.

I had to laugh at that observation. "Well, to be honest, you do come off as a very proud person, and that does annoy me somewhat." I put on my serious face once again. "And what else can you surmise about me, Mr. Wellington?"

"Hmmm…" he pretended to be thinking. "You enjoy your studies at school and are very intelligent."

I smiled at him. Despite my annoyance at him, I did enjoy receiving compliments. I decided I should at least grace him with some sort of a response this time. "I do enjoy my studies. When I was young, I had a private tutor named Tara of whom I was very fond. Along with my parents, she instilled in me a love for learning. When she got married and could no longer be my tutor, my parents sent me off to a private boarding school located about an hour from here every fall. I finally convinced them last year to let me finish my final two years at a school near here where I don't have to board. Now I'm able to live here with my parents during the year and just walk to school every day. I'm so grateful they finally agreed. It's where I met my now best friend Susan and her boyfriend, George. I very much enjoy it."

He raised his eyebrows skeptically. "And you don't miss the rigor of your old school?

I looked down. I could not deny that my studies weren't quite as rigorous at my current school as they were at my old private school. "Well, it definitely is not as difficult at my new school. But sometimes that can be nice. It gives me more time for other things."

"Other things? Like what, may I ask?" He directed his eyes pointedly at me.

His piercing black eyes were a little disconcerting. I squirmed a bit in the rocking chair.

"Well, like my friends and family." I immediately thought of Will and the upcoming school year. "And…other people."

As my eyes met Richard's, it was as if something dawned on him as his face registered some sort of new understanding.

"And is this...person...the reason you don't want to be here right now?"

I looked at him incredulously. How could he have surmised that from what I said? I coughed nervously and looked sheepishly down at my feet. My voice was somewhat apologetic as I spoke. "You could tell that from what I said?"

"Katherine Kensington, I am no fool. I am actually rather perceptive. I could tell as soon as we walked out to the veranda that you didn't really want to be here. It didn't dawn on me until your last comment as to the reason why, but now I know. May I at least know his name?"

I wasn't sure if I should tell him. I didn't fully trust Richard. *Well, a first name couldn't hurt anything,'* I thought.

"His name is Will," I offered quietly.

The amused smile returned to his face. "Will," he repeated after me.

I wasn't sure if it was just my perception or reality, but the way he said the word "Will" sounded like he was posing a challenge.

Chapter Fifteen

Hope's face looked agitated. "Well, Katherine, I hope he soon learned that there was no challenge. Will would win, hands down."

Nicey joined in. "I hope you never had to deal with that man ever again! There's something I don't like about him. Perhaps it's those cold, black eyes..."

Patience looked at her sisters confusedly. "Well, I don't think he sounds *that* bad. I mean, he was handsome and rich. Besides, most men like a challenge." After taking in the glares from her two sisters, she continued on. "Well, it's not like she had to see him after that anyway. We all know that she ended up marrying Will. Isn't that the point of this story? True love and all that mushy gushy love stuff?" She turned to Katherine. "Right, Katherine?" Katherine didn't respond right away. She wasn't sure how to respond.

After a moment of silence, Hope looked pleadingly over at Katherine. "You didn't have to see any more of Richard, right, Katherine? Please tell us you didn't."

It took Katherine a minute to gather together her thoughts.

"Well, ladies, I can't tell you what you want to hear. I did see more of Richard. Unfortunately, I saw a lot more of Richard."

Hope's voice came out somewhat weakly. "And Will? What about Will? You saw more of him, too, right?"

"Yes, I saw more of Will, too." She sighed. "It's kind of complicated. Like I said before I started, this is kind of a long story. I'll get through as much as I can tonight, but it'll take a few more days to tell you the whole story." Her voice wavered a bit. "The next leg of the story is a little painful to tell."

You could have heard a pin drop within the circle of the four ladies. All eyes were on Katherine as she continued her story.

* * * * * * * * *

After Richard's revelation regarding Will, we continued to converse about other things. He told me about his ambitions to take over his father's business and about some of his hobbies. He was somewhat of an outdoorsman, enjoying golfing and hunting in his spare time. He listened attentively as I told stories about growing up and about my friends at school. I realized that underneath the haughty exterior, Richard was actually pretty easy to talk to. I found myself laughing occasionally, and though I hated to admit it, I had a pretty enjoyable afternoon.

I heard the gates opening, and my father rolled up the driveway in his car. He smiled as he got out of the car and headed up the walkway towards us. As he walked up the steps and onto the veranda, he extended his hand towards Richard. "You must be Richard. I'm Michael Kensington, Katherine's father. I've heard such good things about you. It's good to finally meet you."

Richard extended his arm as the two shook hands. "Nice to meet you, Mr. Kensington. You have a beautiful home here." He gestured appreciatively around at the grounds and then ended up looking at me.

"Thank you, Richard. We do enjoy it here. Beauty sure does abound in the South." As my father said that, he looked at me and I got the feeling he was alluding to me in some way. My face flushed a little.

We then heard the dishes clanging in the dining room as the aroma of baked chicken came wafting through the doorway. My father turned towards Richard. "Why don't you come in for dinner? It smells like the cook has prepared an excellent dinner tonight."

As we followed my father through the doorway, I couldn't help but feel annoyed at what had just transpired. It was so different than the time Will had first come over for dinner. Instead of making demeaning comments, my father had instantly accepted Richard and welcomed him in the house like some lost son.

The ensuing dinner continued the same way. My father conversed easily, asking Richard questions about school and his future plans. Occasionally, my father would look over at me pointedly as if to say, *"See what a great young man he is."* I pretended not to see those looks. They only irritated me further.

After dinner, the butler escorted the Wellingtons out to their car after a series of goodbyes. Richard had pulled me aside and commented that he was sure we'd be seeing each other again soon. Though I was frustrated inside, I didn't want to be rude. I told him that I looked forward to it, though that was only half true. True, I didn't mind spending the afternoon with Richard, but I would have much rather spent it with Will.

After the Wellingtons left, I excused myself to my room. I lay on my bed, weary from the day, pulling my pillow over towards the window to catch the beginnings of the sunset. I watched the sky turn from a pale purple to a light orange and finally a brazen pink color. *'That's me right now,'* I thought, *'a brazen pink.'*

My mind churned with the events from the day. I was aggravated by how my parents had plotted against me and had so easily accepted Richard as one of their own. Though Richard had turned out to be somewhat of a charming person, there was something about him that bothered me. It wasn't just his obvious sense of self-importance; it was something else that I couldn't quite place my finger on.

As always, my thoughts turned towards Will. I wondered if Will was watching the same sunset. I wondered if he was thinking about me as I was thinking about him. *'Of course he is,'* I thought. Because Will was the kind of person who stopped to take in the sunset…he was the kind of person who loved me with an intensity I had never experienced prior to him. And no one—not even Mr. Perfect-For-Me-According-To-My-Parents Richard—would ever be able to compete with that love.

"It's too bad, Richard," I said aloud. "You might have had a chance if it weren't for Will. Too bad for you…"

Chapter Sixteen

School started soon enough, the months flying by in my senior year, and Will and I continued to meet each other in the grove a few times a week. My parents did allow me to see Will every once in a while when they realized they didn't have any real reason to keep me at home, and we usually spent that time with Will's father at his house, but we saved any real conversation for the time we spent together in the grove.

In our little clearing in the grove, we talked about everything, from our families to the War in Europe to our ambitions for the future. Our future. Together.

One evening in mid-October, I told Will about my recent realization that I had a real talent for painting. I had been taking an art class at school with a new teacher on staff who, prior to this year, had been teaching at a neighboring district for the past 15 years, and she had told me that I had the most raw talent of any student she had ever come across. I had known that I liked to paint in the past, but I had never really pursued it in the form of a specific painting course.

I took out a small canvas that I had tucked under my coat.

It was a recent painting I had done of the sunset coming across a pond. It was my best painting to date. I loved the way the different hues of the sunset seemed to have a calming effect on the viewer. My parents, who were usually too busy to reflect on much of anything, had even stopped for a few minutes and stared at my painting.

As I turned it towards Will, his eyes first widened with surprise and then turned to admiration as he stared at my painting. He paused for a moment, and then said, "Kate, you never cease to amaze me with your talents. This is unbelievable." He then turned his eyes suspiciously towards me. "How come you never told me you loved to paint?"

I laughed. "I didn't really know I liked it that much myself, nor did I know I had that much of a talent for it. I took a general art class at my old private school, but we focused more on drawing than on painting in that class. So I really didn't know until recently."

He drew me close with the suspicious look still on his face. "Katherine Kensington, what else have you been keeping from me?"

I couldn't help but giggle. I knew he was teasing me, and I liked it. "Hmmm…I guess you'll never know," I teased him back.

He kissed me lightly on the forehead and then on my lips. He gave me a charming smile and said, "I suppose I couldn't get you to part with this…"

I turned the painting over and showed him the message on the back. I had written,

For Will
May our love
Last a lifetime of sunsets
And may we feel its warmth

Across any pond
That may separate us.
Love, Katherine

Will's eyes moved from the caption to mine. "I guess that means yes." He kissed me long and slow, and I wished that kiss would last forever.

Will cleared his throat and got a serious look on his face. "Speaking of ponds that may separate us...I wanted to talk to you about something."

He brought me over to two stumps in the middle of the clearing and sat me down. I didn't like where this conversation was heading.

"I know you and I have discussed the war going on in Europe, and my dad and I have been talking about it a lot at home. If it were up to my dad, he would go over there right now to fight. The only things that are stopping him are his thoughts that he's a little old to fight, for one, and he has been so sick the past few months. I just turned 18 this past February, so I'm old enough to fight, but I don't want to leave my father when he's been so sick, nor do I want to leave you just when we are planning our future together. But I feel this need to... do something more to help. I feel like I can't just stand around watching while innocent people are killed over there." His eyes reflected the torment that had been plaguing him.

My eyes widened with fear. "I hope your dad can shake off this illness soon." I was quiet for a minute as I got the courage up to ask him what I so desperately wanted to know. "Will, are you saying you want to enlist? Do you want to go over and fight?" I fought to keep my voice under control. I wanted desperately to keep Will home where I knew he would be safe. Where we would be safe.

"I'm not sure yet. All I know is that I feel the need to protect the God-given sanctity of life that we all enjoy here. Those Jewish families…I just can't imagine what it's like to be one of them."

Though I wanted to argue with him, in my heart I had to agree. It wasn't fair. People shouldn't be killed because of what race or religion they happened to be, or because their military wasn't as strong as another country's military. Ever since I had known Will, he had always shown himself to be a man of integrity and compassion. However, I wished at the moment that his principles wouldn't be leading him away from me.

He cupped my chin in his hands and looked me in the eyes. "Kate, I haven't decided anything yet. I just wanted you to know what I have been thinking. No matter what happens, one thing is certain."

I looked tearfully into his eyes. "And what's that?"

"I will always love you. And I will always come back for you. Across any pond that may separate us."

I let Will hold me as I cried my anxieties about our future away.

CHAPTER SEVENTEEN

THOUGH I REALLY had no desire to pursue any relationship with Richard, my parents continued to invite the Wellingtons over for social functions. One weekend we had a tennis tournament. Another weekend we had a golf outing. Another weekend we had some family and friends (of the elite type, of course) over for a barbeque.

At every function, I was polite and conversed with Richard and his family. I could sense that Richard was deepening his affections for me, and nothing could have pleased my parents or his parents more than that. They must have missed the fact that the feelings were one-sided and were not being returned by me. My parents knew I still had deep feelings for Will, but I think they figured that the more time I spent with Richard the more I would be convinced he was the better man for me.

At one of our get-togethers in early spring, Richard asked if we could go for a walk alone. Though I enjoyed going for walks, it really wasn't something I wanted to do with *him* at the present moment. I knew he must have something he wanted to say to me, and I was trying to avoid any serious conversations with him. Unable to come up with a valid reason not to, I agreed to go on a short walk with him.

As soon as we started our walk, I tried to steer the conversation towards trivial things like the weather and what our families had been up to lately. As we passed over a little bridge overarching a pond on our property, Richard pulled me aside so I had to stop.

He smiled his little amused smile at me. "Katherine, I didn't ask you to go for a walk so we could talk about the *weather*."

I looked down at the water below us. I didn't like where this was heading, but knew it was inevitable. My eyes met his. "I know."

His eyes clouded over with confusion. "Then what is it?"

My eyes darted down towards the water again. How did I put this into words? How would I tell him that I would never love him? How would I explain that my heart belonged to Will for all eternity?

As it turned out, I didn't have to say anything. My silence spoke volumes to Richard. He was incredibly perceptive, after all.

He looked down at the water as well. His voice was quiet as he spoke. "It's him, isn't it? It's Will…you still love him."

It was more of a statement than a question. My eyes were moist as I faced Richard. I didn't want to hurt him. Though it wasn't the same way as I cared about Will, I had come to care about Richard. "Yes. I still love him. I'm sorry."

We were both silent for a moment as we gazed out over the water. He was the first to break the silence.

"What is it about him that has you so enthralled? Isn't he just a farm boy?" The way he said *farm boy* sounded like venom being extricated from his mouth.

This irked me. He had no right to be so judgmental. I turned to him and looked straight in his eyes. "Yes, he is a farm boy, but not *just* a farm boy. He's a person of faith and courage. And principle," I added, since I didn't think Richard could compete with the last part.

His eyes looked genuinely apologetic. "I didn't take you out here to pick a quarrel, Katherine. I didn't mean it like that." He paused, as if trying to come up with the right words to say. "I just don't understand why you love him so much." Though he didn't say it, Katherine knew what he meant was, *'I just don't understand why you don't love me.'*

It was hard to stay mad at him when he said that. "Oh, Richard, I do care for you. I do. But I can't lie to you. It's just not the same."

What he said next hit me right in the gut. He said it softly as to not anger me. "You have to understand, Katherine, principles or not, your parents will never let you marry Will. He's not the kind of person with whom they would ever allow you to be in the end. You have to know that, Katherine." He didn't say it condescendingly, just honestly. I knew it was the truth.

I swallowed. "I know. But I still love him. And nothing will change that." I wanted to add, *'It won't matter if they won't let me. I'm going to marry him anyways,'* but I didn't want that to get back to my parents' ears.

"I'm not saying you don't love him. I'm just saying that you come from two different worlds. Those two worlds usually don't mix." He paused before continuing. "And I want you to know, Katherine, that when you figure out that love isn't enough to keep you two together, that I'll be here, waiting."

I turned my face away from him. I didn't want him to see the fear written there. Our love had to be enough. It just had to.

Chapter Eighteen

As spring progressed, Will's father's health continued to decline. He had gone to the doctor multiple times, but the doctors couldn't figure out what was wrong with him. His father had asked Will to contact his brother, Will's uncle, about taking in Will's younger brother and sister while he battled his sickness. Will confided in me multiple times in the grove that he was afraid. Very afraid. And I knew it took a lot to frighten Will.

Will gave me a detailed update on his father's health each time we met. To my horror, he explained that during the past few days his father had been coughing up blood. He had also been sleeping more, which was unusual for him. Will also noticed that his father hadn't been eating as much and had been steadily losing weight over the past few weeks. At this pace, Will said, he was afraid his father wouldn't be around much longer. I knew that besides me, Will's father was the most important person in the world to him.

And then it happened. One rainy evening in early May, Will and I had arranged to meet in the grove. I went there after dinner, a little earlier than our agreed-upon time, and as I came into the clearing, Will wasn't there. I realized that I was a little early, so I sat on one of the stumps to wait for him. About 15 minutes passed by, and as I looked at my watch, I noticed that Will was late. He was never late.

Suddenly, it occurred to me that maybe something happened to his father. I got up hastily and headed for the path out of the clearing to head home, thinking that perhaps he had phoned my house while I was here in the grove. I stopped for a second. *'Maybe…'* I thought.

I quickly went back by the stump and opened the little tin that housed the notebook I had brought for messages between the two of us. As I took it out, I saw a note dated with today's date. It was Will's handwriting, though it appeared it was scrawled hastily, as if he were in a hurry. This was also unlike him. It read,

Kate,

If you are here to meet me in the grove and I am not here, then it means I am at home with my father. Things are bad. Really bad. Please come if you can.

Yours always,

Will

I knew I should probably go home first to let my parents know where I was going, but from the sounds of it, I wasn't sure if I was going to have enough time. I decided it was worth incurring their wrath in order to be with Will and his father.

I took the shortcut through the woods. Though I probably had only been walking for less than a half hour, it seemed like an eternity had passed before I reached Will's house.

I didn't even knock. As I entered the house, there was an eerie silence. I went through the kitchen, past the living room, and into Will's father's bedroom. The scene in front of me was enough to break my heart.

Will's father was lying on his bed, looking as pale and gaunt as I had ever seen him. Will was seated on one of their kitchen chairs beside the bed, holding his dad's hand. He looked up as I came in and gave me a small smile. He mouthed, "He's sleeping," before turning his attention back to his dad.

I sat on the edge of the bed, and as I did so, the movement of the mattress stirred Will's father slightly as his eyes flickered with recognition. I could hear his breaths coming out at ragged intervals as he drifted back into sleep.

We stayed like that, the three of us, for quite some time. I turned to whisper something to Will. "Why don't we bring him to the hospital? Maybe they can do something more for him there."

Will adamantly shook his head. "No, we can't. My father specifically told me that he wanted to die at home, not in a hospital. It was his last request, Kate, and I can't deny him that." He heaved a troubled sigh. "Besides, I don't think there's anything they can do for him anyway. He's dying, Kate." A single tear rolled down his cheek.

With that, Will's dad began to stir. I could see that he was trying to open his eyes, though he succeeded only slightly. He was clearing his throat, as if he were trying to say something.

Will said soothingly, "Dad, it's okay. Just go back to sleep. Don't use up your energy by talking to us."

Will's father's voice came out weakly, but audibly. "Son, I…," he seemed to struggle as he gasped in pain. "I want you… to know…I love you…" The last part came out in a whisper. "And love…never…dies…"

And with that, he fell back asleep and never woke up again.

* * *

His funeral was two days later back in Will's hometown near Greenville. It was a well-attended service, with family members and many friends in attendance. As the pastor spoke of Mr. Brenner's kindness and compassion, I couldn't help but feel as if the world were losing one of its best members. All of the things that I loved about Will had been passed down from his father: his fierce sense of right and wrong, his simple but enduring faith, and his love for the people around him.

I watched Will mourn as the casket was lowered into the ground near Will's mother's grave. I grasped his hand as he shook with the emotion he was trying to hold in. With all that was within me, I wished that I could take away Will's pain as he saw his best friend in this world being lowered into the ground.

After the funeral, people began to file out one by one, stopping to give Will their condolences. I saw Will's little brother and sister, who had been living with Will's aunt and uncle since Will's dad had gotten sick, and I gave them a tearful hug before they departed. After the last person left, Will turned to me with resolve in his eyes. "Kate, I know it's going to be hard for the both of us, but I have to go overseas to fight. My dad would have wanted it, and I want it, too. I'm going to enlist tomorrow and leave right after graduation."

I knew this was coming, so I didn't fight it. I didn't have the strength in me at this point anyway. This was something that he needed to do.

There are times in this life when words simply are not enough. As rain began to fall softly from the sky, Will took me into his arms. We stood there embracing, the two of us completely lost in a sea of pain and mourning. Mourning for what Will had lost, and mourning for the uncertainties that lay ahead.

As I thought about Will's father's last words, I secretly hoped that what he said was true. *Love never dies...* If his father was right, our love would survive the turbulent times to come.

* * * * * * * * *

Katherine paused to get a tissue from the table beside her to dab her eyes. As she looked around at the ladies beside her, there wasn't a dry eye there. Even Patience had a tissue and was blowing her nose.

Hope let a little sob escape. "Why do people have to die? It's just not fair."

Nicey patted Hope's leg comfortingly. "We all have to die sometime, Hope. Death is just a part of life." She blew her nose into her tissue.

Patience gave an exasperated look to her two sisters. "Is that what you two are boo-hooing about? I'm crying because Will is leaving." She let out a frustrated sigh. "And just when things were getting good."

Nicey looked over at Patience. "What do you mean by that?" A little smile began to form on her face. "Were you starting to believe in true love or something?"

Patience raised her chin defiantly. "Maybe. But now that's all down the drain. Will is leaving, and now Richard is going to move in on his territory."

"I thought you liked Richard," Hope accused.

"Oh, I was just playing devil's advocate. You two should know I do that sometimes just to get a rise out of you." Patience sighed. "I want Will and Katherine to wind up 'happily ever after' just as much as you two do. And now that's never going to happen."

"Oh, don't be so pessimistic, Patience. She isn't finished with the whole story yet," Nicey chided.

"Yeah, well, it doesn't seem like it's very likely to happen now that he's leaving. He'll probably get killed over in Europe by some crazed Nazi soldier."

Nicey and Hope both gasped. Nicey said, "Patience! I can't believe you sometimes."

Hope added, "Do you really think Katherine would tell us this whole story if Will ended up getting killed? What would that prove about true love?"

"That it doesn't exist, of course! Which, if you recall, was my premise in the first place!" Patience quickly got up and started to head for her room. She turned back to yell something back at us. "I'm going to bed. It's way past my bedtime, anyway!"

The three remaining ladies turned to look at the clock.

"Oh, my!" exclaimed Hope. "It's past ten-thirty. Can you believe it?"

Nicey looked around the room. "We're the only ones out here. I guess we got so enthralled with your story that we didn't notice everyone around us turning in for the night."

Hope yawned. "We keep staying up later and later each night. I think I'm going to sleep in a little bit tomorrow."

Katherine gave the other two a sheepish look. "Sorry, ladies. I try to keep my story as short and sweet as possible, but I keep talking the whole day away!"

Nicey patted Katherine's hand. "Oh, don't you be sorry at all! This is the best entertainment we've all had in years. Patience included."

"Speaking of Patience," Katherine said, "Do you think she's okay? I know you said she gets like this, but she seemed pretty upset."

Hope looked over at Nicey before beginning. "Oh, I think she'll be fine in the morning. She always is a little grumpy at night." Hope giggled to herself. "Well, actually, she's a little grumpy *all* the time, but especially right before bedtime."

"Oh, I think there's a little more to it than that tonight," Nicey reflected. "I think our little ball-of-steam sister is wrestling inside right now. I think she really wants to believe in love, but can't quite forgive Virgil, even after all these years. Actually, I think she can't quite forgive herself."

The three ladies sat in silence for a moment as they mulled over Nicey's last statement. Hope was the first to break the silence. "Well, I think it's time for this gal to get some sleep. Goodnight!" She slowly got up and headed to her room.

Nicey got up as well and stretched. "I know I'll sleep well tonight. Goodnight, Katherine. See you in the morning." She headed off to her room as well.

Katherine sat by herself for a few minutes and reflected on her day. She had gotten quite far in her story, but still had a ways to go. If the three sisters thought today's tale was tragic, they had no idea what was in store for them tomorrow. It was like a small molehill compared to the mountain of tragedy they would soon climb.

'Well,' Katherine thought as she got up and headed to her room, *'Get your hiking boots on and get your sleep, ladies, because tomorrow's going to be a rough climb.'*

CHAPTER NINETEEN

KATHERINE HAD DECIDED not to set an alarm and just let her body wake up when it was rested. Her late-night storytelling had left her physically and emotionally exhausted. She knew her body needed it, and besides that, it wouldn't hurt to sleep in since the other ladies would probably be sleeping in as well.

Katherine slept like a rock all night. When she finally came to, she looked at her alarm clock and realized she had almost overslept past breakfast. It was 7:50, and breakfast would be served in 10 minutes.

She rolled out of bed, got dressed in her walking clothes, splashed a little water on her face, brushed her teeth, and put on a little make-up. She turned her head and did a little self-assessment in the mirror. *'Well, it's not the best I've ever looked, but it'll have to do until I have time to take a walk and a shower after breakfast,'* she thought.

As Katherine entered the commons area, she noticed only one chair was occupied in their little circle of easy chairs. Hope was sitting there, sipping some coffee and looking over the advice columns in the newspaper.

She looked up and smiled as Katherine approached. "Good morning, Katherine." She looked around at all of the empty chairs. "I guess it'll just be the two of us for breakfast this morning. I think the other two are still sleeping. I just got up a little while ago, and I put my ears to their doors when I walked by. I didn't hear a peep."

"Well, I just woke up about ten minutes ago. I haven't slept in that late for years. I must have been really tired," Katherine said as a small yawn escaped.

Hope giggled. "It sounds like you could still use a little more sleep." She looked down at the newspaper. "Look here, Katherine. This one woman named Lucy wrote in to 'Dear Melissa' wondering if she should marry the person her parents want her to marry or the person she wants to marry. Isn't that tragic? She should marry for love, of course. One should always marry for love," she said reflectively.

"Hmmm…" Katherine said. Her eyebrows knitted together in thought.

Hope looked over at her. "What is it? What are you thinking?"

Katherine cleared her throat. "I was thinking that it's not always that clear-cut of a decision. Of course, a person always wants to marry for love, but sometimes other things get in the way. Things a person can't foresee. Things a person can't help from happening." The last few lines came out in a rush.

Hope looked at Katherine as if she were trying to figure out a puzzle. Her eyes flashed as something slowly dawned on her. "Are you talking about Lucy, or are you talking about yourself?" she asked quietly.

Katherine looked down. "I guess a little of both." She sighed and looked out the window at the birds on the birdfeeder outside the window. "You'll see after today."

Hope waited for Katherine to say more, but since she

didn't offer anything else, she changed the subject. "Today is Wednesday. Guess what that means?" She smiled at Katherine excitedly.

With that smile, Katherine guessed it had to be something about John. "Hmmm…today is Wednesday. So that means… only two more days until the big date night," Katherine guessed.

Hope giggled. "You got it! I think that's why I woke up earlier than all of you did today. I'm just so excited!"

"Any more clues as to where he's taking you?" Katherine asked.

Hope sighed contentedly. "Nope, but that's okay with me. I love surprises."

The two chatted about the upcoming date as they ate their breakfast of eggs, toast, and fruit that was served to them.

"Well," Katherine said after finishing her last strawberry, "I wanted to get in a short walk and a shower before starting my story again today."

"That's fine. I don't think the other two will be up for a while anyway. I think I'll just finish up reading this advice column while I wait for them." She smiled guiltily. "I guess I live vicariously through the love lives of these women I read about."

"Not for long," Katherine said. "After Friday, women all across America will want to be reading about you."

Hope blushed. "I sure hope so. I've lived nearly a lifetime waiting for it to happen to me."

Katherine smiled encouragingly at Hope as she got up and headed out the front entrance.

Her body was definitely sluggish after the late night last night. Katherine willed her legs to work, finally falling in a familiar rhythm as she walked on one of the walking paths through the woods on the northeastern side of New Horizons.

She came out of the woods and crossed over onto the road that went by the clearing.

As she entered the grove of trees, she paused for a bit and took in a deep breath of fresh air. The grove always seemed to have its own distinct smell; one of pine needles, wet bark, and various wild flowers that grew intermittently amongst the trees. She walked down the worn path toward her bench and Will's grave.

She let out a weary sigh as she sat on the bench. She rested her fingers on the inscription, closed her eyes, and let the remembrance of Will's love wash over her.

After a few minutes, she opened up her eyes and focused her eyes on Will's grave. She cleared her throat and spoke her thoughts aloud. "I'm here a little later than usual. I got to storytelling last night and got a little carried away, so I couldn't get here until after breakfast this morning." She smiled a rueful little smile. "Anyway, I got to the part of your father's death and funeral where you told me you were leaving for war. There wasn't a dry eye in the place when I finished."

Her eyes misted over a little. "I almost don't want to go back. As soon as Nicey and Patience are up, I'm sure they'll want to hear what happened after you left. This is the part I've been dreading for days. It's the part I haven't told anyone…except for you, that is."

She looked up at the treetops, deep in thought. "I didn't even get to the worst part of the story yesterday, and Patience was upset after that. I'm afraid she'll never forgive me after she hears what happens in today's part of the story." Katherine closed her eyes. "I know it took me most of my lifetime to forgive myself for it."

Katherine ran her fingers over the inscription on the bench one last time. *Will loves Katherine.* She smiled up at the sky. "If I can just make it through today, the rest of the story is a piece of cake." She closed her eyes to pray a prayer that had become familiar to her ever since Will had passed on. "God, give me the strength to make it through today."

With that, she got up and headed back towards New Horizons. The ladies would be waiting.

Chapter Twenty

PATIENCE HAD BEEN watching through the big bay window that faced the front side of New Horizons ever since she had gotten up. Hope had told her that Katherine had gone for a walk and would be back soon. Though Patience hadn't told anyone, she was secretly investigating a mystery that involved Katherine.

It seemed that every time Katherine went for a walk, she entered a little grove of trees just north of New Horizons and didn't come out for at least a half an hour. Sure enough, the same thing happened this morning. She saw Katherine enter the grove of trees, and about a half an hour later, she saw her exit on a different path and head back towards New Horizons.

Patience felt like there was something that she must be missing. It was like she had all the pieces of the puzzle, but just couldn't fit them together. She was about to turn around to head back to the circle of easy chairs with her sisters when something hit her. She looked back out the window towards the grove of trees. "I wonder..." she thought aloud.

She would have to test her new theory out later. There wasn't time for it now. She suppressed a smile as she headed over to her sisters. She sat down and began to work with fervor on her knitting.

Nicey noticed Patience's abrupt beeline for her chair and her sudden interest in her knitting project. As she continued to watch her sister, she saw Patience smiling as she worked and also noticed that Patience hadn't made any mistakes since she started. This was a minor miracle in itself. "Patience, you seem like you're in a good mood this morning. You must have gotten a good night's sleep last night," she commented.

"Why, yes, I did, thank you very much." She looked smugly at her sister. "And I always start out in a good mood every morning. It's just that someone usually ruins it at some point in the day. That's not my fault."

Before Nicey had a chance to comment, Katherine came through the front doors and headed over towards the sisters.

"You're back!" Hope exclaimed. "How was your late morning walk?"

Katherine smiled. "Oh, not bad. It started out a little lethargically, but ended up well. Sometimes it takes a little while to get my blood pumping and my legs moving." She winked at the ladies. "Especially after a late night."

Nicey put her hand on her forehead and closed her eyes. "Don't even talk about last night. I'm still playing catch-up. We'll have to go to bed a little earlier tonight."

"Yes, I don't think my body can make it through another night as late as the last one," Hope added.

"Well, I better start early then, so it doesn't get so late tonight," Katherine said.

"Oh, please do. I am hoping Will comes back to you soon so that you get your happily ever after," Hope prompted.

"I hope it ends better than yesterday," Patience mumbled grumpily.

Nicey glared at Patience. "What happened to your good

mood? No one even did anything, and you are already cranky."

Patience looked offended. "I'm not cranky. I'm merely stating what I'm thinking. It's just that if Katherine here wants me to believe in true love, her story better change for the better pretty soon. Either that or she'll lose an audience member."

Nicey looked apologetically at Katherine. "I'm sorry that Patience is such a party-pooper. Hope and I here will listen to the story no matter what happens." She looked over at Patience. "And no matter what happens, we will continue to believe in the power of love."

Katherine looked down for a second. "Well, I'm afraid it has to get worse before it gets better." She looked directly at Patience. "But I can promise you that if you hear me through to the end, you won't regret it."

Patience seemed to consider it. "I'll try. It's just that I'm not a very patient person by nature, and this is a very long story."

Nicey smiled at Patience. "Well, it's about time you admitted that. It only took you about 70 years!"

Before Patience had a chance to say anything else, Katherine started in on her story.

* * * * * * * * *

As Will had resolved, he left in early June right after graduation. Prior to his departure, we had spent every waking moment that we weren't in school together. My parents didn't even try to stop me this time. I think they figured he would be out of my life soon enough, with either distance separating us from each other or death.

Before Will got into his truck to leave, we leaned on the fence in front of his barn, hand in hand, with my head resting on his shoulder. We sat like that for some time, each thinking that if we said nothing, then perhaps the moment would never come.

He was the first to break the silence. "Kate, just because I'm leaving doesn't mean we have to feel apart. I'll write you. One letter a day until I come back. So even when I'm not here in person, you'll feel my presence through my letters." He smiled at me. "And trust me, I write pretty amazing letters."

Despite the heaviness I felt inside, a small laugh escaped from me. Will could always make me laugh. "What…have you had a lot of practice writing to girls?" I teased him.

His smile widened. "Oh, you know, there was Fanny Mae Bailey, Veronica Manley…" he was about to go onto a third name when I elbowed him.

"I didn't know I had so much competition," I bantered.

His eyes twinkled a little. "Well, I guess I don't have time to write three girls one letter a day each, so I guess you win by default." His voice turned a little more serious. "Trust me, you leave them all in the dust."

"Gee, thanks." I turned to my bag that I had brought along with me. I pulled a very tiny canvas out. "Well, since you've decided on me as your main lady, I have a little something for you to take along with you." I flipped the painting around to reveal a very small, but detailed painting of our little clearing in the grove of trees. I had captured the vibrant greens of the leaves on the trees, the two stumps in the middle of the clearing, and the sun shining down through the tree branches. "I thought that if we couldn't meet in the grove, you could look at the picture each day and pretend that we were meeting together."

He gently took it in his hands as his eyes devoured all of the minute details of the painting. He flipped it over and looked at the dedication on the back. It read,

For Will,

I hope to meet you here
Each day
Until you come back to me
As I know you will…
Love always,
Your Kate

His eyes reflected his gratitude as he turned them back to me. "Thank you, Kate. This will give me something to look forward to each night when things get rough over there." He turned and fished around in his pocket. "And I have something for you."

He took out a necklace with a tiny ring on the end of it. Will turned the ring, and as I looked closely, I read the word *forever* inscribed on the inside of the ring. "Forever," he said as he put it around my neck.

I smiled and ran my finger over the inscription on the ring.

"Now, whenever you look at this, you will remember how long I will love you," he said as he tenderly reached down and kissed me first on the lips and then on the forehead.

He cleared his throat. "There's something else I wanted you to know before I leave." He gestured to the house and the surroundings. "I sold the place last week." As he saw my eyebrows raised in surprise, he kept on going. "A few days before my father died, he told me he had made a will. In it, he left the property to me, since I'm the oldest son, and his remaining possessions to my younger brother and sister, who are living with my aunt and uncle permanently now. I decided that since I was leaving for an undetermined amount of time, it was as good a time as any to sell it. I put the money in a savings account for when I get back home. It's going to be the money you and I can begin a life with when I come back for you." He paused as he slowly ran his fingers through my hair and pulled me close to him. "And I will come back for you. I promise."

I closed my eyes and tried to hold back my tears. I had promised myself that I wouldn't cry in front of him, wanting to spare him any pain that I could. Hoping that my spoken words would will it to happen, I buried my face in Will's chest and whispered, "I believe you."

* * *

True to his word, Will wrote me once a day. Actually, I received a letter the day after he left, so I knew he had sent it before he departed. That one read,

My One-and-Only Kate,

I promised you I'd write you once a day, and I didn't want you to have to wait a few days before you received my first letter. I sent this from my house before we said goodbye.

I hope you understand why I had to leave. Even though leaving you is one of the most difficult things I've ever had to do, I can almost feel my father's approval raining down from above for making this decision. Besides that, I feel that my sacrifice of my time will somehow help our country's cause of liberating the oppressed overseas. I would want someone else to do the same for me if the situation were reversed.

If I haven't told you this lately, I think you're the most amazing person I've ever met. Your love for life, your ready smile, and your belief in me all drive me onward to accomplish the task set before me. I know I have your love and it is enough.

I can't help thinking about what my father said to me before he

passed away: Love never dies. I know that he was probably talking about his love for me, but I think it also applies to our love as well. No matter the distance, no matter what happens, I know beyond a shadow of a doubt that our love will never die. Never. Please believe that.

Counting the days away until I see your smiling face again,

Will

Each day when the mail came, I feverishly read the pages tucked inside the envelope. Will told about his training here in the States, his travel overseas to Europe, stories about the time spent in his unit, and always, in every letter, he expressed how much he missed hearing my voice and how he was counting the days down until he would see me again.

I received one letter every day for four months. And then the letters stopped.

Chapter Twenty-One

At first, I thought that perhaps there had been a little hitch with the mail service and I would get a letter the following day. One day wasn't anything to be alarmed about.

The next day, I nervously awaited the mail coming all morning. As soon as the mail was brought in, I eagerly rummaged through it, hoping to see Will's familiar handwriting. Nothing. I felt a little uneasy inside, but told myself it was nothing to be upset about yet.

After a week, I could convince myself no longer that it had something to do with the postal system. I rummaged through the mail twice every day, hoping for some sort of miracle, but found nothing.

After two weeks, I was beside myself with anxiety. I started to telephone all of Will's relatives for whom I could find numbers, but nobody seemed to know anything. They were all at as much a loss as I was for information.

Shortly after that, as I was mulling things over on the rocking chair on our veranda, an idea occurred to me. At first, everything inside of me wanted to reject my idea, but the more

I thought about it, the more plausible it seemed. The more plausible it seemed, the angrier I began to get inside.

I suddenly got up, stormed inside, and, finding my mother sitting on a chair in the parlor, I turned on her. "Mother, you aren't hiding Will's letters from me, are you?" I saw her surprised reaction, but kept on going. "It's no secret that you and father don't think Will is good enough for me. You haven't been keeping them from me in an attempt to keep us from each other, have you?" I pursed my lips angrily and glared at her from under my furrowed eyebrows.

My mother seemed genuinely taken aback. She put her hand to her chest. "Why Katherine, I can't believe you would think that about me. I would never do that to you."

I wasn't convinced. Now that I had my nerve, I was going to air it all out. "You can't deny that you never liked Will. Admit it. And don't even think of lying to me. I overheard you and father plotting to keep us apart shortly after you met him. You didn't know I was listening, but I was."

This seemed to unnerve my mother a little. It took her a second to gather herself before she spoke again. "I can't deny that your father and I feel that Will isn't right for you. We did decide that we were going to try to limit your time with him. I will admit that. However, it wasn't because we didn't like Will. We both think he's a fine young man in his own right, but we just didn't like him for you. There's a difference." She paused for a moment before continuing. "With that being said, I would never, ever consider taking Will's letters out of the mail and keeping them from you. I'm actually a little hurt that you would even think that I would do that to you." Her eyes began to tear up a little as her eyes met mine.

As I looked into her eyes, I began to soften a little. I even began to feel a little guilty for accusing her. But then, I thought of Will, and I had to be sure before I relented. "Mother, you have to promise on your life that you did not take those letters."

She looked at me, not an ounce of guilt in her eyes. "Katherine, do you honestly think that I could stand by and watch my only child hurting day after day and know that I had caused that pain? If you honestly believe I could do that, then I have not done my job as a parent." Her voice was firm as she spoke again. "I promise, on my life, that I would not do that to you."

As mad as I had been when I first had entered the room, I knew that my mother was speaking the truth. And because I knew she was speaking the truth, I knew that the only other options were imprisonment or death for Will. Nothing else would keep him from me. With that realization fully rearing its head within me, I suddenly broke down and began to cry. My mother got up off of the chair, and without a word, wrapped her arms around me as sobs ripped through my body. We stayed like that for some time, my sobs eventually dying out as my body wearied from emotion.

Shortly after that, I began writing letters to the Department of War searching for any sort of an answer that I could get. About two weeks after my first letter, I received a reply. Unfortunately, it wasn't the answer I was looking for. The reply simply stated that a few people from that regiment, including Will, were not accounted for at that time. They said they were "looking into it" and hoped to have some information soon.

By the time I received the reply from the Department of War, it was over four weeks since Will's last letter. My mind began to consider the worst scenarios. Perhaps he had been killed and nobody had found his remains. Perhaps he was being held hostage somewhere.

In my entire life, I had never felt so helpless. There was literally nothing else that I could think to do. I continued to write letters to Will, hoping they would somehow find him. They weren't getting sent back, so that gave me some hope.

I started to wonder what Will would do if the tables were turned and he were in my situation. I knew what he would do. First, he would never give up hope. Second, he would pray.

And so I began to pray. Every day, I begged God to send Will back to me, safe and sound.

Sometimes I still walked out to our little clearing to air my prayers to God. One day about six weeks after Will's last letter, I sat on one of the stumps in the clearing and looked up at the sky. I couldn't hold it in anymore. I was tired of being ignored.

My eyes teared up as I raised my chin defiantly in the air. "God, if you care about me at all, you will bring Will back to me. You have to. You just have to. Will promised me."

I grabbed the little ring on the chain around my neck and held it up. "See, it says 'forever' on it. Forever. We haven't even had a chance to start our life together. Don't make Will a liar. Please bring him back. Please."

As my tears began to fall freely down my face, I knew that my angry prayers were probably not gaining me any favor with God. Knowing that, I still couldn't keep it from coming out. I just felt so betrayed inside. I tried to soften my voice a little before continuing. "God, Will believes in you so much and has shown me how to trust. I'm trying to trust in you. Please answer me."

As I looked up into the sky one last time, I fully expected to see something that would tell me God was listening. Nothing happened. Perhaps God's silence was an answer. Just not the answer I was looking for.

CHAPTER TWENTY-TWO

HOPE AND NICEY were both blowing their noses as Katherine paused for a moment in her story. Patience was looking off towards the window with an unreadable expression on her face.

"I just didn't expect this," Nicey said. "I thought the hardships you've been hinting at lately were the months of separation you two would have with Will being overseas. I just don't understand why the letters stopped."

"It's just so horrible," Hope sobbed into her tissue. "Why do such bad things happen to good people?"

Patience turned her attention from the window back to the ladies. "I don't understand why this story is going this direction. Will is supposed to go off to war, come back home, and marry Katherine. *That* is what is supposed to happen. *That* is what might convince me to believe in all this love stuff. I just don't understand." She looked back out the window with obvious frustration written all over her face.

Nicey patted Patience on the leg. "She's not done with her

story yet, Patience. We just have to keep listening. It has to get better soon."

"Yeah, that's because it can't get any worse! I thought last night was bad enough. And now this!" Patience crossed her arms with a huff and turned her face away from the rest of the ladies.

Katherine looked sympathetically at Patience, trying to think of something to say, when she saw the New Horizons staff moving around with lunch plates by the kitchen area. A distraction might be just the thing that was needed right now. She cleared her throat to get Patience's attention. "Look, ladies, it's time for lunch already. It looks like soup and sandwiches today."

Patience turned to look towards the kitchen and the sour expression momentarily left her face. She mumbled, "At least lunch looks promising. Unlike this story."

Nicey caught on to Katherine's attempt to distract Patience and added, "Ooh, look Patience. It looks like chicken noodle soup…your favorite."

Hope chimed in, "Just like Mother used to make. I always loved homemade chicken noodle soup days."

Patience sighed, as if signaling that she had given up on being angry in lieu of eating her favorite soup. As the New Horizons staff members brought out trays with the lunches on them, Patience took a big whiff and said, "Well, it may not be Mother's famous chicken noodle soup, but it sure smells good right now."

"I miss Mother," Hope said wistfully as she began to eat her soup. "She really was a wonderful woman."

Nicey looked over at her sister with a sad smile on her face. "I miss her, too. Especially when I eat chicken noodle soup."

Patience looked somewhat exasperated. "Well, I miss her, too, but we don't need to sit around and have a boo-hoo session about it." Her expression took on a bothered look. "Besides, she was kind of hard on me. I think I got spanked the most as a child."

Nicey and Hope both tried to suppress a laugh, but were not successful. Giggles escaped out of their mouths, even with their hands clapped over them.

Patience got an annoyed look on her face. "What are you two laughing about? You know it's true."

Nicey composed herself and said, "Are you trying to get our sympathy? Don't forget that Hope and I grew up with you. I'm not going to argue with you about whether or not you got spanked the most. It's a fact that you did. What you failed to mention is that you *deserved* all those spankings. Actually, you *earned* the spankings, more like." She gave Patience a knowing look. "It's not like Mother just went 'eeny-meeny-miny-moe' and landed on you for the spankings."

Patience stuck her nose in the air. "Well, I know I deserved *some* of them. Just not *all* of them." She looked pointedly at Nicey. "I actually think that you deserved more than you got."

Nicey was a little taken aback. "Me? Are you serious? I was too busy trying to keep you out of trouble to get into trouble myself."

Patience looked to Hope for sympathy. Hope held both of her hands up in a surrendering gesture. "I'm staying out of this one. I just know that Mother and Father were pretty fair about dealing out the discipline."

Patience mumbled, "You would side with her."

Katherine jumped in, attempting to dispel the chance of an argument. "I guess I never asked you ladies much about your mother. What was she like?" She looked over at Patience with a mischievous smile on her face. "Other than an unfair disciplinarian, of course."

Patience ignored Katherine's look and suddenly took more interest in her soup.

Nicey decided she would be the first to answer that question. She looked thoughtfully towards the ceiling, looking as if she were reaching back into the deep recesses of her memory. "Well, if I were to describe Mother in a few words, I would say hardworking and religious."

Hope jumped in to elaborate a bit more. "Yes, she was one of the hardest working women you would ever come across. In fact, she never sat down longer than a few minutes because she was always jumping up to do something. Father would always tell her just to sit down and relax for a while, but she would always say, 'There's just too much to do. Someday when everything on my list is done, then I'll sit down with you for a while.' I guess she never finished checking everything off her list because she never did sit down to relax with Father," Hope concluded.

Nicey smiled in remembrance. "As for being a religious woman, we've already explained to you about the origin of our names being the qualities Mother found in the Bible and wanted for her daughters. Besides that, Mother always made sure we were up and dressed in our finest for church on Sunday. I don't think we missed a Sunday at church."

Hope chimed in again. "And I don't think she missed a day reading her Bible. Every morning when we got up, we would see her finishing up with her 'time alone with God' in her sitting chair by the window that let the morning light come in. She was such a wonderful example."

Patience finished her last spoonful of soup and then decided to add her thoughts into the conversation. "She may have been a 'wonderful example' as you put it, but I think you forgot to add 'unfailingly strict' to your list. I swear, every time I did even the most minute thing wrong, she was there to find it out and punish me for it. I think that besides having five pairs of ears and eyes, she had little spies around to tell her about anything I did. I couldn't get away with anything."

Nicey smiled. "None of us could. You just had more that you were trying to get away with than we did."

Patience's jaw dropped open. "I have no idea what you are talking about. I was a perfect little angel."

Hope giggled. "Just like now, right?"

Patience nodded. "You bet. Just like now."

Nicey turned to Katherine. "Well, I think it's getting a little thick in here. It might be a good time to continue with your story."

Katherine smiled a rueful smile. Part of her wanted to continue, but another part didn't want to revisit the most painful part of her life. She let out a deep sigh, and slowly said, "I left off in the grove where God wasn't answering me…"

* * * * * * * * *

In the following months, my parents showed some compassion and didn't make any comments about Will, but they did not relent on their mission to ensure that Richard had a fair chance at capturing my attention. They invited him over at least once a month for family outings, sometimes with his whole family in attendance and sometimes just him.

At first, I resented Richard's presence, but he was respectful and kept his distance from me. It was as if he could sense my anger radiating from within and wanted to stay out of the wake of it. During those days, he would visit with the adults or challenge my father to a game of tennis. Occasionally, he would come and sit by me, but he never said anything too personal or invasive. He just kept the conversation light and unthreatening.

After a few months, I moved from feeling resentful about

Richard's presence to being neutral about it. I discovered that Richard was actually enjoyable to be around and served as somewhat of a distraction for me from my daily routine of inner torment about Will. While I was with Richard, I wasn't thinking about Will's body being decimated by a grenade. I wasn't wondering if he was undergoing torture after being captured by the enemy. I was able to enjoy life again, albeit tentatively and still somewhat guardedly.

One day when Richard was playing my father in tennis, I decided it was time for me to actually put some effort into at least building my friendship with Richard. As the two approached match point, I said, "I'll play the winner afterwards," knowing full well that Richard would win the next point. Whether it would be Richard actually winning or my father letting him win so he could spend time with me, I'll never know, but Richard was deemed the champion on the last point just as I had predicted.

After shaking hands with my father, Richard approached me with a big smile on his face and said, "So, you decided to give it a chance." What he really was saying, and we both knew it, was *'So you decided to give* me *a chance.'*

I simply nodded and we went on the tennis court to play what would be the first of many matches. I had always enjoyed playing tennis, and played with my father often, but had never played much with anyone my age.

Richard and I went back and forth in the scoring, and he seemed surprised at my agility and ease of play. After we each had won a game apiece, we both had beads of sweat on our foreheads and weren't giving up.

Richard smiled appreciatively at me as I bent down to retrieve a ball before serving. "I didn't realize this would be such a fierce competition. You are better than I thought you would be."

I'm not sure he realized how feisty I could be when challenged.

"Get used to it," I said as I turned my back on him to go to the serving line.

I could hear the obvious satisfaction in his voice as he said, "I will."

As we dueled back and forth, I realized that I hadn't had this much fun since before Will left. Though that thought saddened me for a moment, I realized that I may as well have as much fun enjoying Richard's friendship as I could before Will came back. And I was still counting on Will coming back, no matter what anyone else said.

Richard ended up winning in the last set, and we both walked off the court and collapsed on the lawn in exhaustion. My father, who had been watching the whole match, started laughing at the two of us. I always liked to hear the deep, guttural sound of my father's laugh when he found something especially amusing. I shielded my eyes from the sun and peeked up at my father. "And what, may I ask, is so incredibly funny?"

He looked back down at me and said, "I don't think Richard realizes that you'll give him a run for his money in almost anything. I think he had you pegged for a nice young lady who would let him win pretty easily."

I gave a look of mock outrage. "Well, I don't think it would be very nice of me to just *let* him win. That might inspire a sense of false confidence." I looked pointedly at Richard. "And I sure wouldn't want to do *that*. He doesn't seem to lack anything in that category, anyway."

It was Richard's turn to look outraged. "What? Is it bad for a man to be sure of his abilities? Would you rather I acted meek and were always fishing for a compliment from others to boost my confidence?"

I smiled challengingly at him as I got up to sit in one of the chairs. "Well, you'd have to fish pretty hard to get a compliment out of me."

Richard's jaw dropped. "And what is that supposed to mean?"

"Well, there is a fine line between confidence and arrogance. I haven't decided which one you are." I raised my chin defiantly in the air. "And I don't hand out compliments to just anyone."

My father laughed again and looked over at Richard. "You'll have to battle this one out on your own, Richard." He winked at me. "I'm going to go inside and find your mother. She said she needed help with something. You two have fun out here."

I was pretty sure my mother had said no such thing, but I was in too good of a mood to point that out at the moment. "See you inside," I said as my father walked back towards the house.

Richard got up off the lawn and sat in the chair my father had just vacated. He gave me a mock hurt look and said, "And here I thought you were going to start being nice to me."

I laughed. "I never promised that. I just said I'd play you in tennis. You assumed the rest."

He coughed to clear his throat. "Here I had you pegged for such a nice girl." He shook his head back and forth slowly. "I'll never assume again."

We both sat there for a little while, looking out over the rolling hills beyond the tennis court. My mind wandered to thinking about Will, and I began to feel guilty for having such a good time with Richard. I looked down for a moment as a pang of sadness hit me.

Unfortunately for me, my face could be quite expressive and easy to read. I looked over at Richard, hoping he didn't notice my sudden change of mood. He was studying me quizzically, and all of a sudden he looked away as something dawned on him. After a few moments of silence, Richard cleared his throat and said quietly, "I guess I should also not assume that you are over him."

I didn't need to ask who "him" referred to. I also didn't need to answer. My silence was enough of an answer.

CHAPTER TWENTY-THREE

NICEY PUT HER hand on her chest and closed her eyes. "Oh, poor Richard."

Hope nodded in agreement. "I know. I mean, of course we are all rooting for Will to come back and marry you, but you have to feel sorry for Richard right now. And I don't even like him that much." Her face clouded over in confusion. "I'm not even sure why I don't like him very much, but I don't. It's not like he has even been a bad guy in your story so far."

Patience let out an exasperated sigh. "What do you two mean *poor Richard*? Poor Richard nothing! That man is moving in on Will's lady! What more of a reason do you need not to like him?"

Nicey smiled mischievously at her sister. "Hmmm. All this from the one who in the beginning of the story was telling us that Richard didn't seem so bad because he's rich and handsome. Somehow the tables have turned."

Patience raised her chin into the air. "Well, I already told you I was playing devil's advocate to get a reaction out of you two. Besides, that was before I heard more about Will and how much he loved Katherine. That changes things."

"I'll say it does," Hope agreed.

"I just wish you could get to the part where Will comes back and carries you off into happily ever after," Nicey said. "You *are* going to get to that part, aren't you?"

Katherine didn't want to give the ending of the story away. "You'll see what happens soon enough."

"Well, 'soon enough' isn't soon enough for this lady. This story has been taking forever and keeps getting worse and worse. If it gets any worse I'll have to go poke my eyes out with a pencil just to make myself feel better," Patience mumbled.

Katherine laughed. "Well, I better keep going so you can keep your eyes intact."

* * * * * * * * *

Richard was visiting more frequently now, usually stopping by twice a month instead of the once a month he had been coming by before. Each time he came, he bore a smile on his face that was infectious to me. I began to look forward to his visits, as they served as a healthy distraction for me from the despair I felt about Will's continued absence.

When Richard came, we did a variety of things together. After Richard's discovery that I was quite good at tennis, we often played a match, sometimes with me ending up the victor and sometimes Richard. We ate dinner with my family or with both of our families, depending on if Richard came with his mother and father or unaccompanied. We went to social dances together and danced for hours. We went for walks when the weather was nice and talked about a wide gamut of things.

One subject he avoided was the subject of Will. I think Richard figured that if he never talked about him, then he would simply disappear from my thoughts and my mind.

Unfortunately for Richard, that was not possible. Even

worse, there was a part of me that I had completely closed off from anyone else that could only be accessed by Will. The inner me, the part that truly was able to love another without anything back, the part that had dreamed dreams and painted paintings about how I felt, was unavailable to Richard. Unfortunately for Richard, he would never have the privilege of knowing the real me. He got only the leftovers, but he had no way of knowing that.

And so he continued to pursue me. I could tell that he was falling for me, but I didn't know how to stop it from happening. I needed him for the distraction that he was, but could and would never love him in the way that he wanted me to.

Then there was the separate issue of what happened when Richard wasn't around. When I was with him, he saw the smiling, ready-for-fun-at-the-snap-of-his-fingers Katherine, but when I was at home, I plunged into an almost depression-like state of longing for Will. Inside my mind, I endlessly replayed our conversations we had had together. I remembered each kiss, each embrace, each soft caress of my face.

I also remembered our plans that we had made together. I would pull on the chain that housed the ring inscribed with the word *forever* on it and run my fingers along the inscription. I would close my eyes and pretend that Will had come back. I imagined his proposal and our wedding. I pictured the two of us buying our first home together with the money he had saved from the sale of his dad's house. I pictured the two of us as an old gray-haired couple sitting on the veranda sipping sweet tea on our rocking chairs as we watched the sun set in the west, the pink fingers of the sun magically reaching over to where we were sitting.

And then I would open my eyes. And then the pain would begin once again.

* * * * * * * * *

Katherine was about to say more when the dinner bell rang. She snapped out of her reverie and focused her eyes on the ladies. They all looked completely at a loss. Nicey had her hand on her chest once again and was sighing loudly. Hope had a little tear running down her cheek. Patience had a displeased pout on her face.

No one spoke for a moment. Finally, Hope was able to put her thoughts into words. "I still believe Will will come back for you. I believe he will come back and end all of this pain you are going through."

"Then it will all be worth it. All the pain, all the tears, all the hurt. It will be worth it when Will comes back," Nicey added.

Patience looked appalled. "Worth it? Worth it? Nothing is worth all this misery. Especially not a man. Even a man like Will," she added at the end.

Nicey looked hard at her sister. "You really believe that, Patience? You really don't want Will to come back and marry Katherine?"

Patience looked down at her hands and out the window. Then she turned back to Nicey. "Well, of course I still *want* Will to come back and marry Katherine. I am just saying that all of this waiting isn't worth it." She looked back out the window and repeated quietly, "It's just not worth it." She cleared her throat and said, "I'm going to go to my room for a minute to get something before dinner." Then she abruptly got up and headed for her room.

They all looked after Patience as she made her way to her room. Hope commented, "Hmm. That was odd. She usually doesn't get so emotional."

"Yes, I would say our sister is pretty shaken right now," Nicey added. She turned to look at Katherine. "You see, ever since the whole incident with Virgil happened, Patience pretty much closed herself off to any man. No man would ever be worthy of her attention again. I think that when you talked about closing a part of yourself off to Richard, that awakened a whole slew of bad memories that Patience thought she had successfully hidden from everyone, even herself."

"Yes, and to Patience, no man is worth waiting for. In her opinion, every man just causes pain," Hope reflected.

"And to top it off, Patience closes herself off from *anything* that could potentially be painful. She makes snide comments or uses sarcasm to shield herself from really feeling much of anything," Nicey explained. "I think this story has had too much pain in it lately, and she's not used to dealing with those kinds of feelings. I think it got to be too much for her and she needed to remove herself from the situation. That's why she got up so suddenly to head to her room."

Katherine felt mortified. "So, do you think I should skip over a few things coming up that are painful and just get to the end?" She looked over to Patience's door and let out a big sigh. "Maybe I shouldn't have started this story in the first place."

Hope gasped. "Oh, no, no, no! This is a story that needs to be told. All of it. You can't leave anything out, or else everything you have already told us will be for naught. You are proving to Patience that there is such a thing as true love. She needs to hear it all."

"Yes, and *we* need to hear it all. Don't forget that we have invested in this story, too." Nicey winked at Katherine. "We all need to be reminded of the power of love every once in a while."

"And you are such a great storyteller, Katherine. I haven't heard such a story in…well, my whole life. I just can't wait for the ending," Hope said excitedly.

Katherine couldn't help but smile at their words of

encouragement. "You two are both so sweet. I can't deny that I have enjoyed sharing my story with you, even if some parts have been difficult to tell about." She nodded her head in determination. "Okay, I will finish the story, with all of the details in it. Even the most painful ones. It will make you all appreciate the ending so much more." Her eyes twinkled a little. "And I did promise you all a happy ending."

"You sure did!" Hope agreed.

Nicey looked up as the dinner trays were being passed out. "And look, dinner is served! What great timing."

"Mmm...it looks like beef stew and homemade biscuits. That sounds delicious!" Hope chimed in.

Nicey looked over at Patience's door. "If I'm not mistaken, the smell of the stew will bring Patience out. She always was a good eater."

Sure enough, a few moments later, Patience emerged from her door and headed over towards the ladies. All three of them looked at each other and smiled.

Patience sat down and looked over the tray that had been set out for her. "I could smell the stew and biscuits from my room, even with the door closed. I think all that storytelling has made me famished."

Nicey smiled at her sister. "Did you find whatever it was that you were looking for in your room?"

Patience looked confused for a second, and then remembered that had been her excuse for her abrupt departure into her room. She cleared her throat and mumbled, "Oh, yes. I just needed my sweater." She wrapped it a little more tightly around her. "I was getting a little chilled."

None of the ladies commented on the fact that Patience had already had her sweater on when she went into her room.

Nicey turned to Katherine. "Well, I think it's time to hear

more of this story, Katherine. We all just can't wait to hear how it all turns out."

Patience mumbled in between bites of her stew, "Yeah, we all just can't wait."

Nicey shot her sister a reproachful look and then prodded, "Go on, Katherine. We're listening."

Katherine heaved a big sigh and began once again.

* * * * * * * * *

As I was saying before, Richard was stopping by a lot more frequently now. My mother began making little comments here and there about Richard and his feelings for me. It was getting rather irritating.

One morning, I was sitting on the rocking chair out on the veranda reading *Jane Eyre*, one of my favorite novels, when my mother joined me. This was unusual in itself because my mother was always busy planning social outings with her friends or other such things and rarely took the time to just sit with me.

She took a sip of her tea and looked out over the gardens in the front of the house towards the gate before turning her attention to me. "Richard's mother called to say that he'd probably be stopping over today." Her eyes twinkled with intrigue, hoping that I would share in her excitement over this new development.

I continued to look down at my book. "Hmm," was all that I said.

I could tell that she was hoping for more from me. "Katherine, dear, doesn't that make you happy to hear that he's coming to see you?"

I finally put my book down. It was obvious that she wasn't going to be satisfied until I talked with her.

"Well, Mother, if you must know, I am happy that he's coming to see me. I do enjoy his company."

My mother's eyebrows went up. "And that's it? You simply enjoy his company? There isn't any more to it than that?" she prodded hopefully.

I looked out over the lilies that were blooming over the railing. I was trying to figure out what exactly I should say to her. "Richard and I are…good friends. That's all I consider him at this point. I do love spending time with him and we do have a lot of fun together, but that is where it ends for me." I sighed. "I don't know what else to tell you."

My mother looked disappointed. Actually, she looked a little angry. She cleared her throat, obviously trying to keep her composure. "So what you are telling me is that Richard comes over here multiple times a month to spend time with you and you only consider him a friend?" She huffed a little, gaining steam as she was talking. "You haven't considered the fact that he is looking for more than a 'friend' in you? It hasn't crossed your mind that maybe he considers you as a prospect for his future wife?" Her eyes flashed with anger. "Don't you think that you're leading him on a little if you just consider him a friend?"

I looked down at my feet. What she said was true and I understood why she was angry, but it was never my intention to lead him on. He was just the best distraction that I had at this point to keep my mind off of Will. I looked pleadingly at my mother. "Mother, I do care for Richard, but just not in the way that he cares for me. I can't help that. You can't force yourself to love somebody."

Her expression softened a little. "I'm not saying you need to *force* yourself to love him. I'm just saying you need to be *open* to loving him. You need to give him a chance." She looked back out over the flower garden. "Besides, most of the time love grows over time. You just need to pair yourself up with the most suitable match and leave room for love to grow."

Now it was my turn to get a little angry. "So what you're saying is that it is better to marry someone who appears to be a better 'match' than to marry a person for love? Is that what you are saying?"

My mother seemed a little taken aback. "Well, the way you state it makes it sound so terrible, but to be honest, yes. Love will come. It is better to be with a suitable match than to just be with someone you love who isn't suitable for you." She sensed that I was getting angrier as she spoke, so she tried a different tactic. "Besides, think of all the things you like about Richard. Think of why you like to spend with him." She started counting things off on her fingers. "He's rich, handsome, fun to be around, athletic, and did I mention handsome?" She was trying to get me to laugh, but it wasn't working.

I rolled my eyes. "Mother, I don't think you ever looked past 'rich' when you thought of pairing me up with Richard." I sighed in frustration. "It's just that Richard isn't what I'm looking for in a husband. I don't think I'll ever love him like I want to love the person I'm with forever." I struggled to express myself. "He's just not...he's just not..."

My mother looked down and said so quietly I almost didn't hear her, "He's just not Will."

My eyes widened in surprise. "How did you know?"

My mother reached over the arm of her chair and put her hand on mine in a rare moment of tenderness. "Katherine, you don't have a daughter for as long as I have and not notice how she feels. I know that when you close the door to your bedroom that you cry for Will. I know you are still hoping that he will come back. It's a mother's job to notice these kinds of things."

I looked away as a solitary tear ran down my cheek. I hadn't realized that anyone else knew of my inner torment besides me. I had no words to say.

My mother squeezed my hand and looked directly into my eyes. "Katherine, it's been almost nine months since Will's letters stopped coming. You have to let him go. You have to realize that he's not coming back."

I stifled a sob in my throat. I wouldn't believe what she said. I wouldn't. My next words came out as almost a whisper. "But he promised. He promised he would come back for me."

"Oh, Katherine, I'm sure he fully intended to come back for you, but some promises are meant to be broken. You are meant to be with Richard, not Will."

I took my hand back from underneath hers. She was wrong. I stood up to go inside, but turned when I got to the door. "Will is still coming back for me. You just wait." I said it in a way that sounded like I was trying to convince her, but I knew deep down the one I was trying to convince was myself.

CHAPTER TWENTY-FOUR

TRUE TO HIS word, Richard did stop by later in the day. I had stopped crying a few hours before he came and tried to cover it up with some make-up, but when I looked in the mirror before I went down to meet Richard in the parlor, I could see that my eyes still looked a little red and puffy. I hoped he wouldn't notice. Then I'd have to explain, and I didn't feel like I could do that without crying again.

Richard greeted me in the parlor with a kiss on my cheek, and if he noticed anything out of place, he didn't say anything about it. We sat down on the parlor sofa and small-talked for a little while.

After chit-chatting for a bit, Richard asked if I wanted to go for a long walk. It was a beautiful day outside, a perfect day for walking. I gladly agreed, thinking it would do me some good to get some fresh air and get my mind off of things.

We walked for quite a ways and came up to the place where, if I were walking by myself, I would usually have turned off on the now well-tread path into the grove of trees where Will and I had met so often. I decided that this was a good place to turn around, hoping that Richard wouldn't see the path and want to go that way.

We should have turned around a little earlier, for Richard had already spied and become intrigued by the little path in the grass that led into the grove of trees. He grabbed my hand and tried to pull me along with him. "Katherine, let's go this way. There's a little path here. I am curious as to where it leads."

I stopped dead in my tracks as he tried to lead me to the path. There was no way that Richard would ever step foot with me into that grove of trees. It was sacred ground to me, and I would not defile it with Richard's presence. Over my dead body.

"Richard, I don't really want to go that way. I'd rather we go back to my house and walk over by the pond, if you don't mind," I countered, my voice unusually pleading.

He gave me a puzzled look, perplexed by my unwillingness to do something that he deemed exciting. I usually was game for that sort of thing, but he thankfully didn't force the issue. "That's fine, I guess. If you'd rather, we could walk around your property." He cast one look back at the path. "Another day, perhaps."

As we headed back towards my house, I was noticeably ruffled by the incident. Richard cleared his throat. "Ah, is there something wrong, Katherine? You seem…upset."

I turned to him and forced a smile. "Um, no, I'm fine. I just didn't feel like walking into the trees. You know, bugs and that sort of thing. I just didn't want to risk it," I said convincingly.

His eyebrows shot up as he considered this. "Ah, yes, the bugs. They can be bad this time of year."

We headed back towards my place and made our way to the bridge that overlooked the pond behind my house. We both stopped there, leaning against the railing and looking out over the water.

We stood for a few moments in silence, each lost in our own thoughts, when Richard turned to me and grabbed both of my hands. He turned me towards him. I got an uneasy feeling as my heart started beating like a drum within my chest.

Richard looked right in my eyes. "Katherine, we've been seeing a lot of each other lately, and I want you to know how special you've become to me. You've become this sort of light for me that illuminates my days, and I look forward to each and every moment that we get to spend together."

If I were anybody else but me, I would have thought his words were incredibly romantic and would have swooned upon hearing them. As it was, my heart began to sink lower and lower in my chest with every passing word.

He then got down on one knee. I wanted to scream, *'No! Please don't! Get up!'*, but no words came out of my mouth.

He pulled a black box out of his pocket and looked up at me. "Katherine, I've known you for long enough to know that you are the person with whom I want to spend the rest of my life. You're beautiful, intelligent, adventurous, witty, and you have my heart. When I picture my future, the only person I see with me is you." He paused for a second and then continued. "If you would do me the honor, I would like to ask you to be my wife."

He then looked up expectantly, and for a while no words came to my lips. Finally, through my tears, I said quietly, "Oh, Richard. I do care for you. I really do. But not in the way you want me to." I turned back to the railing on the bridge as Richard slowly got up. "You don't understand. A part of me is broken and can't be fixed. There's a part of me that I will never be able to give to you because I gave it to someone else. I just can't…love you in the way that you want to be loved. I simply can't."

Richard was quiet for a few minutes. Finally, he said,

"Katherine, I'm not asking you to love me in that way yet. I know you are still…dealing with some things. If you care for me at all, you will say yes and give us a chance."

What could I say to that? I did care about him, but not like I cared about Will. "Richard, I just can't say yes. I still…I still…"

Richard's eyes clouded over as he began to understand. "You still love Will. You are still hoping he will come back for you."

I couldn't meet his eyes. All I could muster was a small, "Yes."

Richard grabbed my hands and turned me towards him once again. "Katherine, I don't know how else to say this, but Will is not coming back. He's been gone for a year now. The last time you heard anything from him was nine months ago." I wasn't going to ask him how he knew that. No doubt my mother had informed him. "He's not coming back, Katherine, and you have to move on. It's time to let him go and give someone else a chance."

He paused for a moment, letting that sink in. "Now, I'm not taking this as a 'no', just a 'not yet'. I am a persistent fellow, and when I want something, I don't give up. I'm still going to be here when you realize that I'm right in saying that the best thing is to say yes to me. You've admitted that you care about me. You will grow to love me more. I know you will. Just give us a chance."

That's the same thing my mother had said. *'Your love will grow. Give it a chance.'* Was that possible? Could love grow for someone whom you presently never thought you could love?

As we stood there, hand in hand, I wondered for the first time if that were truly possible. Is that what my mother had done? How about Richard's mother? Was this how the rest of the world operated? Did other people just find the person who was the best 'match' on paper and hope their love would grow?

Was I one lonely ship in the midst of an ocean of hope in feeling that a person should marry for love? If so, I wasn't sure if that one lonely ship was going to survive against all of the other battleships out there waiting to take it down.

* * * * * * * * *

"You are not the only ship who believes a person should marry for love. I believe that, too. A lot of people believe that," Hope offered through misty eyes.

"I know that now, but at the time, it seemed as if I was the only one who felt that way. It seemed everyone around me married for other reasons," Katherine said with a little shrug of her shoulders.

"I married Henry for love," Nicey reflected. "Of course, he was also a good match on paper, but we were definitely in love when we married. We stayed that way the whole time until he… passed away. Oh, how I loved that man." She got a little teary-eyed just remembering.

"Oh, stop your fussing. Henry wasn't anyone worth crying about," Patience said, exasperation written all over her face. "Besides, we're not talking about you and Henry, we're talking about Will and Katherine."

"I know, but I just thought my story reinforced what Katherine was thinking," Nicey said, defending herself.

"Yes, you and Henry were definitely in love," Hope affirmed. Her eyes looked to the ground a little sheepishly. "If I'm being honest, I always was a little jealous of you and Henry for finding each other and having so much happiness. I always wanted that for myself."

"Well, maybe you will still find love," Katherine commented as she looked over at John across the room.

Hope turned a little crimson in the face. "I hope so," she said shyly. "I guess time will tell."

"More like this Friday will tell!" Katherine winked at Hope.

"Oh, I'm getting more and more nervous every day. If I'm already this nervous, what will I be like on Friday?" Hope looked over at John. "I probably will just stand there and not be able to say anything at all. Oh, I hope I don't embarrass myself."

"Knowing you, you probably will," Patience muttered.

"Oh, hush up, Miss Crabby-Pants. Who asked for your opinion?" Nicey scolded.

"I don't need to be asked. I just offer my wisdom freely. Take it or leave it." Patience continued on before Nicey had a chance to say anything. "Besides, dates are always awkward. Someone, either the guy or the girl, always ends up saying or doing something embarrassing. That's the nature of dating." She leaned in more closely and gave the ladies an all-knowing look. "And that's why I don't date."

Nicey rolled her eyes. "And that's too bad. I'm sure there would be men lined up to date such a likable, good-natured person."

Before Patience could retort, Hope interjected. "Well, I'm willing to risk it." Her voice was determined. "Even if I end up doing something embarrassing, it's worth it because at least I'm putting myself out there. At least I'm giving it a chance."

Nicey patted her sister's hand. "Yes, you are giving it a chance, dear. And I'm sure it will turn out well this time." She raised her eyebrows and sat back in her chair. "I have a good feeling about this one, Hope."

"We all do," Katherine added.

They all looked at Patience, expecting her to chip in some encouragement. "Oh, yes. Yay, rah rah. We all have a *great* feeling about this one," she said, somewhat sarcastically.

Nicey looked at her watch. "Goodness, it's almost 8:00. Let's hear a little more of your story before we all head off to bed."

Katherine smiled. "I'll try to get through as much as I can, but I will have to finish up some tomorrow. Otherwise, we'll be up all night!"

"Oh, I don't think we're young enough for that anymore." Hope giggled. "Tell a little tonight, and that will leave us in suspense for the ending tomorrow."

"I vote for putting us all out of our misery and ending it tonight, but I'm sure I'm outnumbered on that one," Patience said.

Nicey gave her sister a look and then turned to Katherine. "Go ahead. You decide how much to tell tonight, and we'll *all* be satisfied with that."

Before Patience had a chance to reply, Katherine started in on her story once again.

* * * * * * * * *

My parents must have known about the proposal because they hinted about it at dinner that evening after Richard had gone home. As we passed around the platters of roast duck, potatoes, and roasted vegetables and began eating, both of my parents attempted to glean any information they could out of me about my afternoon with Richard.

My father started it off. "So, Katherine, what did you and Richard end up doing this afternoon? You were gone for a few hours."

I really didn't want to talk about it. The pain of it all still hadn't worn off, and I was hoping we could talk about something else. Maybe if I just gave them some surface answers and then changed the subject, they would be satisfied. "We went for a long walk out back behind the house. It was nice. What did you two do today?"

My mother chimed in. "Oh, we just did the usual. Your father was puttering around his office, always working, and I was doing some planning for the next benefit." She changed the subject back to me. "So what did you and Richard discuss on your walk?" She looked at me expectantly.

My eyes went down to the food on my plate. How did I answer this one? "Well, we talked about his job and…the weather…and how our families are doing."

"Anything else in particular?" my mother prodded.

There was obviously no way around the subject. I was just going to have to say it. "Actually, Richard proposed to me."

A little squeal escaped from my mother, and my father had a huge smile on his face. "And what did you say in return, Katherine?" she asked.

I coughed and looked back down at my plate. "I haven't given him a definite answer yet. I'm still considering it." Actually, I had given him an answer, but he didn't like it and said it wasn't a "no," just a "not yet." I didn't want to explain all of that to my parents though.

My father's smile lessened, but was still evident. "Well, we both think Richard is an excellent young man, a perfect fit for you. I mean, you two obviously get along well, he's a rather good-looking young man, and he's determined to make something of himself. When you consider all of those things, what is there really to consider?"

I didn't really have an answer to give them. They wouldn't understand anyway. They wouldn't understand that Will really got me, the real me, and reached me in a place that no one else ever could. They wouldn't understand that even though Richard met every item on their checklist, he still wasn't the one with whom I wanted to spend my life.

When my mother saw that I wasn't responding, she chimed in. "Well, at least you didn't say no. It is a big decision, and we know you've been dealing with some other stuff lately." By other stuff, they meant Will, but they didn't want to say his name. She reached over and patted my hand. "We know you'll come to the right decision."

Even though I hadn't eaten very much, I asked if I could be excused and went up to my room. I flopped on my bed and buried my face into my pillow. I wanted to hate my parents, but knew they were just doing what they thought was best for me.

Although I didn't want to admit it, it was nice to feel their approval. The whole time I had been with Will, I felt a constant tension between my parents and me. Since Will had been gone and I had been spending time with Richard, it was as if their approval had been raining down on me. Not only did they approve, but all of the people around them did, too. I hated that it felt good.

Little bits of my parents' conversation at dinner floated around in my head. *"Richard is determined to make something of himself,"* my father had said. Will had been determined, too, but his "making something of himself" didn't include the life of luxury that my parents wanted for me. *"We know you'll come to the right decision,"* was my mother's last comment. Was it the right decision, considering the circumstances? Was Will ever going to come back? Was a promise worth waiting for when I hadn't heard from him in over nine months? If Will were dead, which I was finally admitting to myself was a possibility, wouldn't he want me to move on and marry someone else?

I pulled out the little ring out from underneath my blouse and ran my finger over the word *forever*. I knew that Will would love me forever and I him, but if he died, what was I to do? Remain single forever? Forever hope that he would come back for me until I ended up a lonely, disappointed old woman?

I made a deal with myself. I would wait six more months to give time for Will to come back to me, at which it would be 18 months since he left for overseas. If, at the end of the six months, Will had not come back, I would say yes to Richard.

* * *

The six-month cut-off date loomed over my head like a death sentence waiting to be carried out. As each month passed by, I felt more and more anxious. It was one thing to actually think about my deal with myself and another to actually act on it.

Richard and I continued to see each other, and he acted as charming as ever towards me. If his pride had been wounded by the proposal attempt and he felt any sense of frustration, it never showed in his demeanor towards me. It was like the proposal had never happened, although we both knew inside that it had.

When I was by myself, I continued to walk to the grove and spend time there. It was there that I felt the closest to Will. I wrote down the things that I wanted to say to Will on the notebook inside the tin. My most recent entry read,

My Long-Lost Love,

Please come back to me. I would wait forever if I knew you were truly coming back, but it's the not knowing that is killing me now. Day by day the pressure mounts to give up hope of you ever coming home. Richard continues to pursue me, and though he hasn't said anything as of late, I know inside that he is waiting for an answer. It's an answer I hope to never have to give, if you'll only come back to me and save me from the life my parents and society have destined me to live. It's you and only you who I really want, the only one I've wanted from the beginning. I'd give up the money, the approval of my parents, the life of luxury for the life of pure, simple love that we would have together.

The time has almost run out before I need to give my answer. If that day comes, and you have not been able to make it back, know that I will always love you, and I will know that you are the only one who would ever be able to love me in the way that reaches every part of me, down to my very soul.

Forever Yours,

Katherine

Shortly after I had written that last entry, my own self-imposed six-month time limit had expired. I knew what I had to do.

I visited the grove one last time and sat on one of the stumps in the clearing. I slowly raised my hands to my neck and found the clasp on the back of my necklace. I undid the clasp and took off my necklace. I sat there with the necklace in my hands, running my finger along the ring's inscription. *Forever. Forever.* "Goodbye, forever. Goodbye, Will," I whispered tearfully as I placed the necklace into the tin with the notepad.

Richard came over later that day. And then, eighteen months after Will had left for overseas, I finally said yes to Richard.

* * * * * * * * *

"What? What did you say?" Patience exploded in fury. "That can't be what happened. I think that you are remembering incorrectly and are making a mistake. Take it back. That's not what happened." She was almost shouting now.

"Shh! You're going to wake up the rest of the residents! They have all gone to bed!" Nicey chided her sister.

Hope jumped in. "Patience, Katherine promised us a happy ending, so that can't be the end of it. You just have to have a little faith."

"Faith? Faith? That's what I've had ever since she started this story. And now whatever shred of faith I had is gone. I can't bear to listen to any more. I'm going to bed." She stomped off to her room and was about to slam her door when she remembered everyone else was sleeping. Instead, she turned one last time to give the ladies all a dirty look and then closed the door quietly.

They thought that was it, but the door opened shortly after and an arm came out with a "Do not disturb" sign that was hung on the doorknob.

All three ladies just looked at each other. Hope said, "Golly, do you think she will come back tomorrow to hear the ending?"

"Oh, I think she's just blowing off some steam. I think she'll cool off by tomorrow morning and come out to hear the rest." Nicey was still looking at the "Do not disturb" sign that was currently in its last phases of swinging back and forth.

"I sure hope so. She needs to hear the ending." There was some urgency in Hope's voice when she said the last part.

"Well, if she doesn't come out by 10:00 tomorrow morning, I'll go in and get her," Nicey determined.

"I sure wouldn't want to be in that room when you do that," Hope said, wide-eyed at the prospect of it.

"She's hearing the end of the story, whether I have to drag her out of her room or not," Nicey replied.

Hope looked at the clock and yawned. "It's after nine. This lady needs to go get her beauty sleep." She looked down sheepishly. "I'll need as much as I can get for Friday night!"

"Oh, you'll be beautiful. Especially after we get done with you," Katherine promised.

"I hope so," Hope blushed. "Well, goodnight ladies!" She started making her way to her room.

"Goodnight all," Nicey said as she got up and went to her room.

"Goodnight," Katherine called after the ladies. She decided to just sit in her chair for a few moments by herself. She felt too tired to move. All of this storytelling about the most difficult part of her life was beyond exhausting.

Finally, she forced herself to get up and headed off to her room, hoping that the ending tomorrow was something the ladies would feel was worth the wait. She knew it had been for her.

CHAPTER TWENTY-FIVE

SURPRISINGLY, THE FIRST one up on Thursday morning was none other than Patience. She was up at 6:00, before any of the other ladies had even stepped foot out of their doors. She woke up early because she had some investigating to do.

She had been up much of the prior night thinking about Katherine's story, and suddenly realized something about Katherine that she had never thought of. Katherine had never told any of the ladies her last name. Of course, none of them had ever asked, but nonetheless, she realized that if she could somehow learn Katherine's last name, then she would be able to figure out the ending of the story before Katherine ever told it to them. She wouldn't have to wait all day just to hear the rest of the story.

Plan A was to look in Katherine's mailbox out in the main lobby. Each resident had a small box where their mail was placed each day. Perhaps Katherine didn't get her mail the prior day and Patience could get her hands on a letter addressed to Katherine to learn of her last name. She strolled over to the mailboxes and looked around to make sure no one else was watching. A few residents were up already. She saw John reading the morning newspaper over by the window sipping some coffee. He looked preoccupied with the front page, so he wouldn't notice anything amiss. The other two residents who were up were sitting at a table chatting with each other on the far side of the room.

Patience nonchalantly went over to the K's, and thought how unlucky it was that New Horizons, in an effort to make their care more personal, had organized the mailboxes by first name only instead of with last names. She found Katherine's box, but when she stooped to look inside of it, there was nothing there. Katherine must have picked up her mail yesterday, and it was too early for today's mail to come. "Drats," Patience muttered.

Patience then looked towards the front desk. "Time for Plan B," she whispered under her breath. Patience put a big smile on her face and headed towards Barb, the lady who was at the front desk most mornings.

Barb noticed Patience right away. "Why, hello Patience. My, you're up early. And look how chipper you are this morning."

"Hi, Barb." She made her smile bigger. "You know me, I just couldn't wait to get the day started." She paused for a second, thinking of some excuse that would be plausible to get Katherine's last name. "Barb, I was going to write our new resident, Katherine, a thank you note for something nice she did for me recently, but I wanted to add her last name on the outside envelope to make it look more official. The only problem is that I actually don't know her last name. Is there any way that I could get that from you?" Patience smiled a big, innocent smile at Barb.

Barb's face clouded over in confusion. Patience didn't seem like the kind of person who wrote thank you notes. She didn't even seem like the type of person to notice something for which to be thankful. She asked, "And what did Katherine do for you that was so nice?"

Patience had to think on her feet. "Well, she's just been so encouraging lately to me when I've been feeling down, and I want her to know that I'm thankful for it." That was the best she could come up with. She hoped it would convince her.

Barb seemed as if she was deliberating for a second, and then her face broke into a smile. "Why, Patience, I do believe you are turning over a new leaf. Look at you, noticing when other people do nice things for you." She lowered her voice a little. "Well, I'm probably not supposed to share people's personal information, but a last name isn't that personal, so I'll do it. Her last name is Brenner."

Patience got a big smile on her face. "Thank you, Barb. That's exactly what I needed to hear."

Patience went to sit down in her chair and started working away on her knitting project. She was humming a little tune when Katherine came out of her room at 6:30 to go for her morning walk.

Katherine did a double-take when she saw Patience already up and humming a cheerful tune while she knitted. Patience was never up this early. And she most certainly never hummed. She nodded and said good morning to Patience and headed towards the door.

As Katherine went out to go on her daily walk, Patience suddenly abandoned her post at her chair and moved over to the windows facing the front entrance. "One mystery solved, and now on to the second one," she muttered as she watched Katherine head towards the trails northeast of New Horizons. About twenty minutes later, she saw Katherine come out of the north side of the trails and head towards the grove of trees that she always went into on her walks. As usual, she spent about a half hour in the grove of trees and then headed back towards the building. "Ah hah! Just as I suspected. I know where you go every day. And I know who you married in the end. I have it all figured out."

"You have what all figured out?" Patience heard Nicey's voice behind her and whipped her head around.

"Oh, nothing," Patience said as she quickly walked over to her chair and picked up her knitting project.

Nicey looked out the window. "Now what, or who, are you spying on?" She saw Katherine walking towards the front doors and turned back to her sister. "Oh, I see. You are spying on our Katherine, huh? Is that why you are up so early? I thought I might have to drag you out of bed this morning."

"I just felt like getting up early," Patience said in her own defense. "And I just happened to look out the window when I saw Katherine walking. I can't help that."

"Uh huh. I'm sure." Nicey's voice was dripping with sarcasm. "And what, may I ask, do you have all figured out? Are you going to share that?"

"Just wait. You will see," Patience said mysteriously. "All will become clear in a little while."

"Hmm. I guess we'll see about that." Before Nicey had a chance to say anything else, Katherine came through the front doors.

Katherine saw Nicey as she came in. "Good morning, Nicey. I see you're up early, too."

Nicey looked towards Patience. "Yes, but not up as early as someone else over here." She lowered her voice a little. "I think that same someone was spying on you just a little bit ago."

Katherine's eyes widened. She mouthed, "Me?" and Nicey nodded. Patience pretended not to notice anything and was all of a sudden awfully busy with her knitting project.

Before they could say anything else, Hope's door opened and she came out, yawning and stretching in her doorway and then heading over to the ladies. "Good morning!" She yawned again. "Oh, I just couldn't sleep. Between thinking about your story, Katherine, and being nervous about my date tomorrow, I think I barely slept a wink!" She flopped down in her chair tiredly and laid her head on a pillow.

"Well, I slept perfectly well. I even got up early because I just couldn't wait to start my day," Patience said cheerfully.

Katherine and Hope looked at each other with bewildered looks on their faces. Nicey piped in, "Oh, I don't think you even need to ask, ladies. I think I know why my dear sister here was up so early and why she is so chipper." She paused dramatically before continuing. "Patience here has become a self-appointed investigator of our very own Katherine. I came out of my room just in time to hear Patience say, 'I have it all figured out.' Now what she has all figured out, I'm not sure, but I do know she was looking out the front windows at Katherine on her walk as she said it. Supposedly, it will all 'become clear,' at least according to Patience."

Patience got a smug look on her face. "Okay, I was doing some investigating, I admit it. And I must say, I am pretty good at finding out information when I set my mind to it!" She looked at all of the ladies as they were sitting down in their seats, interested to hear what she had to say. "And I just know that I am right about two very important things." She stopped there, enjoying the fact that she had everyone's full attention.

Nicey let out an exasperated sigh. "Well? What exactly did you figure out, little Miss Investigator?"

Patience gave her sister an annoyed look. "I don't like your tone. Maybe I won't share what I found out." She crossed her arms in front of her in mock annoyance and looked out the window.

Hope looked at the other two and then back at Patience. "Oh, come on Patience. You know we all want to hear what you have to say."

"I want Nicey to say she's sorry first," she said in a self-righteous tone.

Nicey sighed once again and said, "I'm sorry, Patience, for being snippy with you." She was going to say something else, but then decided better of it.

"That's better," Patience said. "Anyway, as I was saying, I found out two things. I'll share one now, and the second one I need to do a little more investigating about before I share it." She looked around to see if the ladies were interested. Their eyes were all glued on her. She turned her attention to Katherine. "Well, for one, I found out your last name is Brenner. Is that correct?"

"Why, yes, as a matter of fact, it is," Katherine answered.

The smug look had returned to Patience's face. "So that means that you didn't marry Richard, and that you do end up marrying Will instead. I mean, you told us in the beginning of the story that Will's last name was Brenner, so if your last name is Brenner now, then logically that means you two got married instead of you and Richard. Will does come back to you after all." She crossed her arms and leaned back in her chair, obviously pleased with herself for her findings.

"So then what happens with Richard?" Nicey prodded. "You must have a theory about that, too. I mean, Will can't just come back for Katherine without something happening with Richard."

Patience looked up in the air as if she was thinking. "Well, I haven't figured all of that out quite yet. I do have two theories that are plausible. One, Will comes back before Katherine and Richard get married, Katherine breaks off the engagement with Richard, and then Will and Katherine get married and live happily ever after. Richard then falls in love with someone else down the line and gets married."

"And what's theory number two?" Nicey asked skeptically.

"Theory number two is that Will comes back, murders Richard, and then Katherine is free to marry him instead." Patience leaned back in her chair once again, obviously happy with her findings.

"What? That's the most preposterous thing I've ever heard!" Nicey exclaimed. "Does Will seem like the type of man who would murder someone? Seriously, Patience!"

Patience got a little defensive. "Well, he would have just come back from war. Richard is an enemy, so maybe he just does him in."

Hope's jaw dropped open, astonished at her sister. "Patience, people know the difference between war and real life. And like Nicey said, Will is just not the type of person who murders someone else. Besides, if he did murder Richard, how would he marry Katherine? He would be in jail!"

"Well, Will is a pretty smart guy. Maybe he made it look like it wasn't a murder. Maybe he staged it like a suicide or something. Or a natural accident. You never know."

"Oh, enough of this!" Nicey said. She turned to Katherine. "Why don't you tell us how much, if anything, is true of what Patience supposedly found out."

"Well, a couple of things were right." Katherine smiled at Patience.

Patience smirked. "What did I tell you?" Then, under her breath, she added, "I bet it's the murder part that's right."

Katherine laughed. "I best dispel that rumor right away. No, Will did not kill Richard. But Will does come back."

Patience looked over at Nicey. "See, I told you he comes back before she marries Richard."

Katherine sighed. "But not before I married Richard."

Now all three sisters looked at her and said, "What?" simultaneously.

"I did marry Richard first. Six months after I said yes to Richard's proposal, Richard and I were married."

The three sisters were at a loss of what to say. Patience finally said, "So then how does Will fit back in to this story?"

"Well, it's all rather complicated, but before you go to bed tonight, you shall have the rest of the story," Katherine promised.

"It's about time," Patience muttered.

* * * * * * * * *

As I was saying, six months later, during the summer of 1946 when I was 20 years old, Richard and I were married. I was happy, but it was a reserved sort of happy. I couldn't help but wish, deep down, that it were Will up there with me in front of the preacher instead of Richard. I was banking on the fact that, just as my mother had said, my love would grow for Richard in the coming years.

Either way, it was the social event of the season. My parents, being from an established family with old Southern money, spent a ridiculous amount on the whole ordeal. My mother had spent the six months preceding the wedding planning everything down to the smallest detail. There were flowers decorating every row of chairs, every table at the reception, every person who my mother deemed in need of a flower, which seemed to be at least half of the guests in attendance. The food was impeccable, the weather was gorgeous, and the bride and groom appeared to be a glowing couple with a bright future ahead of them.

After the wedding was over, Richard and I moved into a home we picked out together in his hometown of Lexington. It was difficult to leave the town in which I had grown up and say goodbye to my parents, but they would only be a little ways away and I knew we would see them often.

Our new home would be somewhat of a solace to me for a couple of different reasons. For one, it was in Lexington, which was altogether a new place for me. In Lexington were no reminders of Will or the life we had together, so it was a place where essentially I could have a fresh start. Second, I really did love our new home. It had an extensive garden where I could sit outside on the benches and let nature perform its magic on me. There was also a room overlooking the gardens that I thought I could use as a painting studio. I hadn't painted since Will had left, and I was aching to try it again.

I hadn't told Richard anything about my painting, since that was something I shared with Will. After we had settled in, I bought some canvas and some painting supplies in town and decided that it was time for me to paint again. While Richard was gone at work, I set up my easel, mixed my paints, and sat down to begin. I held my brush up to the canvas, but nothing came to me. One hour passed. Two hours. When I heard the door open as Richard came home, I still had a blank canvas. For some reason, I had lost my inspiration to paint. I took the canvas down, put my painting supplies away, and didn't paint for years to come.

The first few years of our marriage were happy in the way that Richard and I were comfortable with each other. We had established our routines of normal domestic life. I had made some friends my age in Lexington, and we got together often during the days to pass the time while our husbands were at work. When Richard got home, we ate dinner together that our cook had prepared. I actually had wanted to try my hand at cooking and not hire someone, but Richard wouldn't hear of it. He seemed surprised that I would even suggest it. We spent the evenings with friends at different social functions or at home. We still played tennis together and went for walks. We enjoyed each other's company.

With all that being said, I still did not love him in the way that I had hoped to love my spouse. I did love him in a way, but it wasn't the same way I had loved Will. I had loved Will with every part of me; nothing was hidden from him. He knew the real me, whereas Richard just thought he knew me. I had hoped my love for Richard would grow to equal what I had felt with Will, but unfortunately, that didn't happen. It saddened me at times, but I made a choice to be happy and love Richard in what capacity I could.

We saw my parents at holidays and other various occasions. One time, about three years after Richard and I had gotten married, we were visiting my parents for the Easter holiday. It was a gorgeous day out; the flowers were blooming, the grass was turning green, and the birds were singing their little warbles to each other across a warm current of spring air. I asked Richard if he wanted to go for a walk, but he said I should go on ahead while he chatted with my parents a bit more.

I went through our front gates and decided to go wherever my feet took me. I found myself walking in a familiar direction, towards the grove that held the clearing. I hadn't been there since I had taken off my necklace and said goodbye to Will before getting engaged to Richard. I noticed that the path was a little overgrown, but still visible. I entered the grove and made my way to the clearing, and looked up at the sunshine cascading down on me. I closed my eyes, basking in the sunlight, letting it rain down on me for a moment.

I sat down on the stump and leaned down to pick up the little tin. I slowly removed the lid, took out the notebook, and read my last message to Will. As I read, my earlier pain resurfaced and a solitary tear escaped down my cheek. I pulled out the necklace, and, catering to my impulses, put it around my neck. I ran my finger over the word *forever* once again. Tilting my chin towards the sky, I closed my eyes and remembered the last time I had been here with Will.

When I lowered my eyes back to ground level, I had the strangest sensation that Will was actually there with me. It was as if he was there but I couldn't see him. I spoke his name into the trees, "Will..."

Instead of hearing Will's voice, it was Richard's I heard from behind me. "Will is dead, Katherine. Remember?"

I jumped a little and turned around. His voice had sounded odd and cold. I wasn't sure how long he had been there. I really didn't want to know.

"I decided I wanted to catch up with you on your walk and followed you shortly after you left your parents' house. You can imagine my surprise when you went into this grove of trees that you were so reluctant to go into the last time we walked this way together."

He approached me and I encased my hand around the necklace protectively. "And what do we have here?" he asked menacingly. He picked up the little tin with the notebook in it. I could see him paging through past few entries. His eyebrows went up in surprise as he read. Then his eyes lit up as if something dawned on him. "So, is this your special little place where you and Will met together?"

I didn't say anything. My silence let him know that he was right. He threw the tin to the side and I moved to pick it up. As I did, my hand came off of the necklace. Richard intercepted me before I got to the tin. His hand went to the necklace, and he ripped it right off of my neck. My hand went to my throat and my eyes widened in surprise.

He turned around and looked at the little ring on the end of the necklace. "Forever," he read, his voice dripping with disgust. "It was bad enough when I had to compete with Will when he was alive. Now I have to compete with him when he's dead, too." He threw the necklace as far as he could into the brush at the edge of the trees.

Before I could say or do anything, he grabbed my hand and yanked me towards the path on which we had separately come. "Come with me, my *loyal* wife. You can think about Will all you want, but it's not going to bring him back. Remember, it's my ring you have around your finger. *My* ring."

He pulled me all the way back to my parents' house, and, upon our entry into the front gates, opened the car door for me and all but pushed me in. "I'm going to go say goodbye to your parents and let them know that we're leaving. Oh, and I'll be sure to wish them a 'Happy Easter' so that I can share my overflowing joy with them." He slammed the car door and walked up the veranda steps into the house.

As I sat there in the car by myself, a million thoughts raced through my head. What had I been thinking to go into our clearing and put that necklace around my neck? Now Richard knew about the clearing, and, as long as he lived, he would never let me go back there again. I felt a pang of guilt as I wondered if I had been unfaithful in any way. Could I help it if I still missed Will? Were my memories of Will supposed to just disappear when I married Richard? Was it wrong to think of Will sometimes? Then my moment of guilt turned to anger. Richard had no right to react the way he did. He knew upon marrying me that I still missed Will, but I was giving him a chance. He could have tried to understand how I felt instead of raging at me. My anger then turned to fear. For the first time since I had married Richard, I felt afraid of him. What would our marriage be like now? Would I live in fear of my husband for the rest of my life?

I didn't have long to ponder that last thought because I saw Richard storm out of my parents' front door and over to the car. He put the key into the ignition, but before starting the car, he turned to me. "You will never visit that grove of trees again. And mark my word, I will erase each and every memory you have of Will, one by one, if it kills me." He then started the car, and, as we drove in silence all the way home, I was left to wonder exactly what erasing each and every memory of Will would entail for Richard. I decided I didn't want to know.

CHAPTER TWENTY-SIX

HOPE GASPED AT Katherine's last statement. "Oh, how scary! Katherine, I feel afraid for you. I knew there was something I didn't like about Richard. I just knew it."

"No woman should have to live in fear of her husband," Nicey added emphatically. "No woman."

"Oooh, if Richard were here right now, I would give him a piece of my mind," Patience said. "Threatening his own wife like that. Maybe now you all understand why I always say all men are pigs."

"Well, I don't know about all men. You like Will. He's not a pig," Nicey reminded Patience.

"Yes, but he still let Katherine down by not coming back." Patience looked at Katherine and then added, "Well, not yet at least." Hope looked angry. "I am so mad at Richard right now that I almost want Will to come back and do Richard in. Just like Patience said earlier." She crossed her arms and let out a frustrated sigh.

Patience laughed. "See? My theory wasn't so bad after all.

Even Hope, who is usually the nicest one out of all of us, wants Richard to die."

"I can't say that I wouldn't mind if Richard got out of the picture permanently," Nicey said reflectively. "Although I don't want Will to be the one to do it."

"Why don't you tell us what happens, Katherine, instead of us all guessing about it," Hope prompted.

"And make something very bad happen to Richard, even if that's not really what happened," Patience added.

"Oh, something bad does happen to Richard. I don't even have to make that up. You will see." All eyes were glued on Katherine as she began once again.

* * * * * * * * *

After that long car ride home, the period of what I call "The Coldness" set in. This is where Richard turned into the harsh person I suspected was inside all along, but couldn't quite put into words. I should have known from those jet-black eyes that The Coldness lay within.

Where formerly Richard had been pleasant and what I would consider loving towards me, he now acted as though any kindness by him was forced. He kept track of my every movement, wanting to know where I was going and when I would be back. Where he used to converse with me freely, he now only communicated with me when necessary and replied to me with one word answers. When in public, he acted the part of the doting husband, but as soon as we were in the car on our way home, he turned back into the Richard who had now made my life a living hell.

Richard also began drinking heavily. Whereas he used to be what I would consider a social drinker, he now drank from the time he got home until the time he went to bed. At one point, while in one of his drunken rages, he came into the library where I was reading and spewed out, "A man of principle, huh? He wanted to fight for the Jews overseas, huh? Well, look where it got him!" He turned around, slammed the door, and went back to get another drink.

As he had promised earlier, Richard was on a mission to erase my memories of Will. He searched through my things, looking for anything that Will had given me and promptly disposed of it. One day, when I was gone visiting a friend, he found Will's letters that I had hidden under the bed and he burned them. I figured that out when I saw something on the edge of the fireplace that looked familiar, and saw it was a piece of a letter that had escaped the burning.

He also became obsessed with having a child, since he thought that might make me forget about Will and focus on our baby. He was hoping for a baby boy to carry forward the family name. The problem was that I wasn't getting pregnant. This enraged Richard even further.

One day he exploded on me. "What is wrong with you? It's like your body refuses to have anything to do with me, just like your mind has already done." He glowered at me. "I'm right, aren't I? You just simply don't want to have anything to do with me." He looked away for a moment. "We could have been happy, you know. Now look at what you've turned me into." He hovered over me like he was going to hit me, but then decided better of it. "No, don't worry, my darling. I wouldn't hit you. I'm not going to give you any real reason to divorce me. I'm yours forever." He laughed a bitter laugh and left the room.

And so that was my life for the next four years. I lived as a prisoner in my own home. I told no one about what was going on, partially because I blamed myself for provoking The Coldness with the incident in the grove, and partially because I didn't think anyone could really help my with my predicament.

Richard never technically did anything that would be considered abusive and would be grounds for divorce; he simply made me feel helpless and hopeless.

Richard soon began leaving during the evenings to go out with friends to drink. I suspected he was seeing other women, although there was no physical evidence of any such thing. One would think that would bother a woman, but in this case, I welcomed the reprieve. I was simply happy that he was out and left me to myself instead of verbally torturing me in his drunken stupors. He no longer bothered with trying for a boy, since he had figured that if it hadn't happened yet, it was never going to happen.

It was during this time that I began to paint again. As soon as Richard left for the evenings, I pulled out my canvas and supplies and discovered that I could paint out of my pain. My paintings were different than the ones I used to paint for Will; now I used dark hues and painted in a more abstract style rather than the tangible outdoor scenes I used to paint.

They were beautiful in a more subdued sort of way; they made you reflect on the sad things that happened in your life instead of the happy ones. Life was composed of both the light and dark hues. On one palette were the dark things in life: loss, broken relationships, and unspeakable pain represented by the blacks, blues, purples, and grays. The other palette held the light hues, the good things in life: smiles, laughter, hope, and love represented by yellows, greens, pinks, and oranges. If a person never had been affected by the dark hues, the light ones wouldn't seem so beautiful. I was in the process of learning that lesson.

I decided to bring one of my best paintings to the art gallery in town to see if they might consider buying it. Jennifer, the receptionist at the front desk, brought me in to a back room to see Mr. Santini, the owner. He was an Italian man of about thirty years old with curly black hair and a charming accent. I turned the painting around and placed it on an easel in the corner of the room so he could get a better look at it. He put his hand up to his chin and walked back and forth, as if assessing the worth of the painting. He didn't say anything for quite some time. I thought that probably meant he wasn't interested, so I started walking towards the easel to take the painting down.

He held his hand out as if to stop me. "No, no. Just leave it there. I love what you've done with the colors here." He pointed a part of the painting that seemed to be the focal point to which the viewer's eyes were naturally drawn. "It makes me think of the time I lost my only sister in an automobile accident, but it's a cathartic kind of sadness."

I cleared my throat. "Is it something that you would like to have in your gallery?" I asked.

He thought for minute. "Yes. Most definitely yes. In fact, I would like to see more of your work." He paused for a moment. "How about two hundred dollars?"

My eyebrows shot up in surprise. "Two hundred dollars?" I repeated.

He looked displeased. "What? Is that not enough? I suppose I could give you a bit more, but you are a beginning artist. I usually only pay around fifty dollars for new artists' work. You have quite the talent. How long did you say you've been painting?"

"I started painting in high school, about six years ago. I've been painting on and off since then." Then I added, "And two hundred dollars is plenty. That was more than I planned on getting. I wasn't even sure if you would like it."

"Like it? I love it," he said enthusiastically. "I've been wanting to add something a little different to my gallery. This will be just the thing!" He took my hand and led me back towards the front desk. "Come! Jennifer will get you the two hundred dollars, and I am hoping to see more of you in the future. Goodbye now."

He talked to Jennifer for a moment and then left us for the back room. After he was out of earshot, Jennifer said, "Wow, your artwork must be impressive. I've never seen Mr. Santini give out this much money for someone's first sale." She handed me the money and I was on my way.

In the months to come, I continued to paint and sold Mr. Santini quite a few more of my paintings. They turned out to be his top sellers in the gallery. I couldn't believe that people actually wanted to buy my paintings. Will and few others had told me I had some talent, but I thought they were just saying that to be nice.

And then it happened. One evening when Richard was out, I was painting in what I now dubbed my art studio when I heard a knock at the door. The front gates were open because Richard was still out, and I had no idea who it could be. I peeked out the front window by the door and saw a police car in the driveway and an officer at the door. My first thought was that Richard had gotten in trouble in one of his drunken fits, though he had plenty of money and that would usually buy him out of any predicament.

As I opened the door, I recognized the officer as one whom I had seen in town on an earlier occasion. He pulled off his cap and held it out in front of him. "Good evening, ma'am. Are you Mrs. Wellington?"

I cleared my throat. "Yes. How may I help you?"

"Well, I'm sorry to tell you this, ma'am, but there's been an accident involving Mr. Wellington."

I paused for a moment. "What kind of an accident?"

"Well, it seems that Mr. Wellington may have had too much to drink and drove into a tree when on his way home."

My brow furrowed in confusion. I didn't know what to think. "Is he okay?" was all I could think to ask.

The officer paused before answering. "Well, this is hard for me to tell you this, but he was killed on impact. I'm so sorry, ma'am." He looked down at his feet, as if giving me some privacy. Realizing that I didn't have anything to say, he then continued on. "If you need any assistance or have any questions, ma'am, feel free to give us a call at the station. I'm really very sorry." With that, he turned around and headed back to his car.

I slowly closed the door. Tears began falling down my face, but they weren't tears of sadness; they were tears of joy. I was finally free. Free! I ran upstairs and jumped on my bed as a myriad of thoughts went through my head. Richard couldn't hold me as a prisoner in his own house any longer. I could move anywhere I wanted to. I never had to feel afraid anymore.

I looked out my window and up at the sky. Not that God had caused this to happen, but I felt that He had somehow heard my prayers desperately calling out for help. I looked up and whispered, "Thank you." I lay back down on my bed, and, for the first time in years, slept the sleep of a woman free from anxiety and worry.

* * * * * * * * *

"Now, that's better," Patience said. "He finally got what he deserved. I kind of wish it had been a more painful death, though, instead of dying on impact. Maybe getting zapped by a lightning bolt or being burned at the stake would have been a little more satisfying."

"Patience!" Nicey scolded. "It is not very Christian to want bad things to happen to other people. It's God's job to get vengeance, not ours."

"Well, He did get it. He made Richard run into a tree,"

Patience argued. "Besides, you can't deny that you wanted something to happen to Richard. You even said so yourself earlier." She looked around at the other ladies to try to get some affirmation.

Nicey coughed and changed the subject. "Oh, it looks as if they are bringing out the lunch trays." She looked at the tray that was set down in front of her. "Mmm, chicken pasta salad and whole grain rolls. Delicious!"

The other ladies soon received their trays and began eating. After a few minutes, Hope turned to Katherine. "Katherine, you just have to tell us the ending now. I was going to let you finish your whole meal before asking, but I just can't wait any longer. Maybe you can tell us the rest of the story while we finish eating?" She looked like a little child asking her mother for something that she wanted very badly.

A little laugh escaped from Katherine. "Yes, I suppose we could do that. I know you ladies have been waiting for days for this ending."

"Yeah, but it felt like years," Patience mumbled as she took a bite of her salad.

* * * * * * * * *

After the funeral, where I acted the part of the grieving widow, I put the house up for sale and decided to move back to Summerville. My parents had recently moved to Charleston since most of my dad's business was there, but I didn't mind moving back and living by myself. I wanted to be back in a place that reminded me of Will, even if he was gone.

I decided to rent a small apartment at the edge of downtown Summerville that had a large patio window overlooking a pond to the east. I figured the sunsets over the pond would give me some inspiration for my painting. I kept a small amount of furniture from the house, but sold the rest at an auction. I didn't need much at this point in my life. I had my freedom, and that was enough.

After settling in, I decided to go for a walk and visit the little grove of trees that housed our little clearing. It had always been a place where I could sit and reflect, and I felt that I could use a little time for reflection.

I had heard through the grapevine that the old owners of the property that housed the grove of trees had grown old and sold it to a new owner. Will had known the prior owner and had asked permission to be on his property long ago, so I hoped the new owner wouldn't mind the intrusion.

It was a good two-mile walk from the apartment. I had worked up a good sweat by the time I got to the little path that led into the clearing. It was a little overgrown, but it looked as if someone had been walking on it recently. Maybe someone else had discovered the magic of the grove and had been visiting it.

As I walked into the grove and approached the clearing in the middle, I went slowly, as if taking it all in for the first time. The branches of the trees arched over me as the sunlight filtered into the clearing. I tilted my chin upward, closing my eyes, letting the quiet of the place restore my soul.

I then made my way over to one of the stumps in the middle and sat down. I looked down by my feet, and saw the little tin below. That was strange. The last time I had been in the clearing was when Richard had followed me and had thrown the tin in a fit of temper. The cover had been replaced on the tin and it had been put back in its original spot by the stump. Had someone else stumbled upon it and put it back out of consideration for its owners?

I was about to open the tin when I heard a twig snap behind me. I looked to the back of the grove and saw the silhouette of a man. I dropped the tin and stood up. I couldn't quite see who it was, but I figured it was the new owner.

I decided to apologize before he could get mad about me being on his property. "Hello? I'm sorry I'm on your property. The old owners used to let me come here, and I guess I just couldn't resist coming back one last time." I paused to see if he would answer, but he didn't say anything. "I'll just be going now."

I turned to leave and heard the man say something. "You don't need to leave. You could stay here with me, Kate."

I whipped my head back around. I knew that voice. It sounded like…no, it couldn't be. No one called me Kate but Will.

We both started walking towards each other. As he got closer, I stopped. It looked like Will, but it couldn't be. It just couldn't.

I stood there for what seemed like forever, my feet locked in disbelief. My eyes must be playing tricks on me. Will just couldn't be alive. He just couldn't possibly be here right now.

"Will?" My voice came out weakly. I felt dizzy, as if I could faint at any moment.

He started walking towards me more quickly now. He stopped when he got to me, and I started spitting out incoherent things. Finally, real words started coming out of my mouth. "How… where…is that really you? How…is this possible? Will?"

That old familiar smile graced his face. He put his arms around me and pulled me close to him. "It's me, Kate. I'm real. I promise."

As he held me to him, tears started running down my face. This wasn't possible. But he sounded real. He felt real. Was I dreaming?

He loosened his hold on me and we stood face to face. "Will,

I thought you were dead. Everyone did. I don't understand how you are here right now."

He looked down at me tenderly. "I know. I thought I was going to die, too." He paused for a moment, as if the memory was a painful one. "I was a prisoner of war for three years. Every day I waited for death but prayed for life. I'm not sure why, but the main guard, a German fellow, liked me. He kept me around for some reason I couldn't understand. Unfortunately for him, when I gained his trust, he didn't watch me as closely. I figured a way out of the make-shift prison, taking a few of my guys with me. We made it out alive."

I looked at him in disbelief. "And when did you get back here? Was it after…"

He sighed. "Yes, you and Richard were already married. I didn't want to make your life worse by letting you know I was still alive and back here, so I just laid low. I figured someday you would be free from him, and I made a vow to wait until that day, even if it didn't happen until I was old and gray. Fortunately, I didn't have to wait that long. Six years isn't anything to wait when you really love someone."

I looked down sheepishly. "I wish I had waited." I looked back up and a tear ran down my cheek. "I mean, if I had only known you were alive, I would have waited forever. I believed for so long that you were coming back, but then I just gave up hope and married Richard. I'm so sorry."

He kissed my forehead in that spot he always used to kiss me. He took one hand, cupped it under my chin, and tilted my face up to his so his eyes were looking directly into mine. "You have nothing to be sorry for, Kate. There's no way you could have known. I think anyone would have done the same in your shoes, especially with the pressure your parents were putting on you to marry Richard."

"I know, but you would have waited if the situation were reversed," I said quietly. "You would have waited for me."

He smiled at me. "But I didn't have Richard pursuing me, did I."

I knew what he said was true, but my heart still ached with the knowledge that I could have been with Will instead of Richard. "It's strange," I said. "Even when I thought you were dead, I still felt like you were here with me sometimes. There was one time in particular, about four years ago, when I came here and had this overwhelming feeling that you were physically in this place. I even said your name…but then Richard came." I looked away as I recalled the pain that day had caused in my life.

Will reached down in his pocket to get something. I could barely believe my eyes when I saw what he was retrieving. It was the necklace he had given me before he left with the little ring inscribed with *forever* on the end. Richard had ripped it off my neck and thrown it in the brush the last time I was here, but somehow Will now had it in his hands, fully repaired with a new clasp on it. He reached up and put it around my neck. "I was there. That was shortly after I had come back, and I was watching from the edge of the grove of trees. It took all that was in me not to step in and beat the living tar out of Richard when I saw how he treated you. The only thing stopping me was that it would have made your life ten times worse if both you and Richard knew I was alive. I couldn't live with myself if I had caused that to happen."

He paused as he looked out towards the brush were Richard had thrown my necklace. "After you two left, it took me a while to find where he had thrown the necklace, but I found it. I have a friend who makes and repairs jewelry, and he fixed it for me. I put it in my pocket every day and walk down here, hoping to run into you."

I looked around the grove towards where I had first seen Will. "I thought you were the new owner of the place coming to kick me off your property at first." A little giggle escaped my mouth." I just couldn't believe it when I heard your voice coming out of who I thought was the owner's mouth. I couldn't believe it was you."

"Well, you were right about one thing," he said. "The new owner was coming down to see who was in his grove of trees."

I started looking around, thinking he meant the new owner was somewhere around us. Then it dawned on me what he meant. "Wait a minute," I said. "*You* own this property now?"

His smile widened. "Yep. I bought it with the money I saved from selling my father's house after he died." He then looked down and got something out of his shirt pocket. "Actually, if you're willing, *we* are the new owners of this place." He grabbed my hands, got down on one knee, and looked up into my eyes. "Kate, I've never loved anyone as much as I love you. It was the thought of you that kept me alive all those years when I was imprisoned overseas. You're the only one I want to spend the rest of my life with. *Forever.*" He emphasized the last word, and I reached up to run my finger over the inscription on my necklace.

I smiled through the tears running down my face. "Forever," I repeated. "Yes, forever!" I shouted as Will stood up, lifted me in the air above him and twirled me around. When he put me down, he cradled my head in his hand and pulled me towards him for the kiss my lips had been aching for since the day he left.

* * * * * * * * *

As Katherine ended her story and looked around at the

ladies, all three had tears running down their faces. A few tears had even escaped Patience's eyes.

"Oh, how I do love those kisses," Hope said as she sniffled and wiped her nose with a tissue.

"And I love those happy endings!" Nicey exclaimed, a smile coming through her tears. She turned to Patience. "See, I told you if you stuck around long enough, you would get to hear the happy ending. I don't know how you can't believe in true love after that story."

"Well, that proves I was right," Patience said.

Nicey looked confused. "Right about what? You never believed in true love before the story started."

Patience gave her sister an exasperated look. "No, not about that. The jury is still out on that subject. I was right about Katherine marrying Will. Just not exactly in the order I thought she would," Patience said.

"Well, of course she married Will. What kind of a story would it have been if she ended up with Richard the rest of her life?" Nicey retorted.

"So there is hope for all of us. Even me," Hope said, looking over at John across the room.

Katherine smiled at Hope. "Yes, there is always hope for all of us. Never give up on hope. I learned that lesson the hard way."

"Speaking of Hope, we have to help you get some stuff ready for your date tomorrow," Nicey said to her sister, her eyebrows going up excitedly.

"Oh, yes. That's tomorrow! Katherine's story was a good distraction for me from thinking about it so much, but now that her story's done, that's all I will be thinking about! Oh, I won't sleep a wink tonight!" she exclaimed nervously.

Nicey patted her sister on the leg. "You'll be fine. We'll get you all ready to go, and then all you have to do is be yourself.

I don't know how he can't go crazy about you if you do that. Especially with the way we will have you looking tomorrow night."

"I do hope it all goes well," Hope sighed. "Let's go to my room so you can help me decide on my outfit." As she got up to head to her room, Nicey and Katherine trailed behind her.

Nicey turned around before she went in Hope's door. "Patience, are you coming, or are you going to sit out here by yourself?"

"Oh, why not?" Patience mumbled before getting up. "She's going to go on her date whether I help or not, so I may as well."

Nicey and Katherine each took one of Patience's hands and pulled her in the door, and all four ladies spent the next few hours giggling and getting Hope prepared for her big date.

CHAPTER TWENTY-SEVEN

THE NEXT MORNING, Patience woke up early and knocked on both of her sisters' doors. They both came to their doors with sleepy expressions on their faces.

"What do you want?" Nicey said. "Why are you up so early again? Are you up to something?"

Patience kept her voice to a whisper. "Remember when I said that I had found out two things yesterday, but I only shared one because I still had more investigating to do on the second one? Well, I want you two to help me in my investigation."

Nicey looked at her sister suspiciously. "Is it something that will make Katherine mad?"

Patience shot her sister an innocent look. "No! If we do it right, Katherine won't even know we're there."

"Where's there?" Hope asked, yawning into her hand.

"Why don't you two go get ready and meet me out in the commons area in fifteen minutes? I will explain the plan there."

Before her sisters could ask any more questions, Patience

had turned around and was heading towards her seat in the commons area.

Fifteen minutes later, both Nicey and Hope emerged from their rooms and came out to join Patience in the easy chairs.

"So?" Nicey prodded Patience. "What's the big plan? What's this all about?"

Patience looked around. "I have to talk fast because Katherine usually gets up about this time." She looked to the right and to the left. "You know the clearing in the grove of trees that Katherine talked about in her story so much? The one where Will came back and proposed? Well, I think I know where it is." She paused for dramatic effect, letting it sink in with her sisters.

Both Hope's and Nicey's eyes widened. "You do? Where?" Hope asked.

"I'll show you in a little bit. We'll have to wait until Katherine comes out to go on her walk, and then I'll take you there. But we'll have to be fast! We'll only have a few minutes there before Katherine comes. At least if my theory is correct," Patience said mysteriously.

As if on cue, Katherine emerged from her room in her walking clothes. Patience saw her, turned to her sisters, and urgently whispered, "Quick! Pick up your knitting projects! Otherwise, we might look suspicious just sitting here!"

All three ladies simultaneously picked up their knitting projects as Katherine started walking towards the front door. As she passed, she saw the ladies there and stopped with a confused look on her face. "My, you three are all up early…and knitting already! How did you all sleep?"

"Fine," all three said at once, none of them stopping to look up as they knit like their hands were on fire.

When Katherine realized none of them were going to offer

any more, she said, "Well, I'm off for my daily walk. I'll see you ladies at breakfast."

As she went out the door and headed over to the trails to the northeast of New Horizons, Patience ran to the bay window. She watched Katherine walking for a while, and then looked up towards the sky. "Hmm, it looks like it might rain. We might get wet. Oh well, it's all in the quest for truth!" she said dramatically.

As soon as Patience saw Katherine disappear into the trails, she said, "Come on! We have to go now!"

Nicey and Hope followed Patience, trying to keep up with her rapid pace. After a few minutes, Hope said, "Geez, Patience, I haven't seen you move this fast since that time your hair caught on fire when you were a teenager."

Nicey stopped for a second, trying to regain her breath. "Yeah, and remember that I'm your oldest sister and not quite as spry as you are. Slow down a little."

"We can't slow down. We don't have time for that. Besides, we're almost there!" Patience yelled back to them.

Sure enough, the ladies soon approached a grove of trees. They saw a little path on the left side heading into the trees. "So this is where…" Hope said.

"I think so," Patience responded, reading her sister's mind.

Patience took the lead on the path, followed by Hope and then Nicey in the back, still trying to catch her breath. As they entered the grove of trees, they all noticed a little clearing on the right.

"I can't believe it!" Hope exclaimed. "I didn't know the grove was this close to us!"

"This whole time we've been here, we've never known it was right under our noses," Nicey added in.

The three ladies approached the clearing, and all three looked up and let the sunlight filtering through the trees hit their faces. "This place is truly magical," Hope said.

As they walked in further, they saw a bench and a gravestone. Nicey went over to the bench and saw an inscription on the front. She ran her fingers over it and read it aloud, "Will loves Katherine." She looked at the other two. "It looks like Will made this for Katherine. How beautiful."

As Nicey sat on the bench, Patience and Hope walked over to the gravestone. Patience cleared her throat and read, "William Michael Brenner. February 3, 1925-April 25, 2001. Man of faith, courage and heart. Loving husband and friend." All three ladies just looked at each other for a few minutes in reverent awe.

Patience broke the silence when she looked at the time on her watch. "Quickly, ladies! Katherine will be here any moment! She always comes out of the trails and heads this way. We can't be in here when she comes. Let's hide behind the brush in those trees over there."

All three sisters scurried behind the brush in the trees, hidden from view if a person were in the clearing. Shortly after, Katherine emerged into the clearing from a path on the other side of the grove of trees. She went to the gravestone, paused for a moment, and sat on the bench.

She looked up into the sky, as if she were talking directly to Will in heaven. "Well, I finished the story yesterday. All of it. I had never told the whole story to anyone. Well, except for you, of course. I think they liked it."

She paused, sighing for a moment before beginning again. "The only problem is that I told the story to answer their question of whether true love exists or not. I was trying to prove to Patience that true love really does exist, but I'm not sure if she believes it, even after the whole story was finished. I think it encouraged Hope to give love a chance, though, so I feel like it was worth it. She has her date tonight with John, you know." She smiled. "I have a feeling it's going to go well. Hope deserves to find love, even at this age." She looked down for a moment. "I didn't deserve your love after giving up on it, but you gave me a second chance. You never gave up on me. You were way more than I deserved."

Katherine was silent for a few minutes, and as she sat on her bench running her fingers over Will's inscription, it began to rain softly. She got up, went to the middle of the clearing, raised her hands to her side, and tilted her face towards the sky, letting the rain fall softly on her face. She began to twirl in the rain, like a little girl twirling around in a ballerina costume in front of her father.

As the sisters watched this scene, a solitary tear escaped from Patience's eye. Nicey grabbed Patience's hand and whispered, "What is it, Patience?"

Patience sniffled a little. "Okay, okay, I admit it. I believe." She sighed. "I believe in true love."

"What?" Hope said. She couldn't believe it.

"Oh, you heard me. I'm not saying it again." She turned and looked at both of her sisters. "And you better not get any ideas about hooking me up with anyone just yet. I still think *most* men are pigs."

Nicey and Hope smiled at each other and then turned to look one last time at Katherine, who was still twirling, the rain falling freely down her face, a woman who had loved fully and had been loved fully in return.

Manufactured By: RR Donnelley
                     Momence, IL USA
                     January, 2011